LEGO

NINJAGO

Masters of Spinjitzu

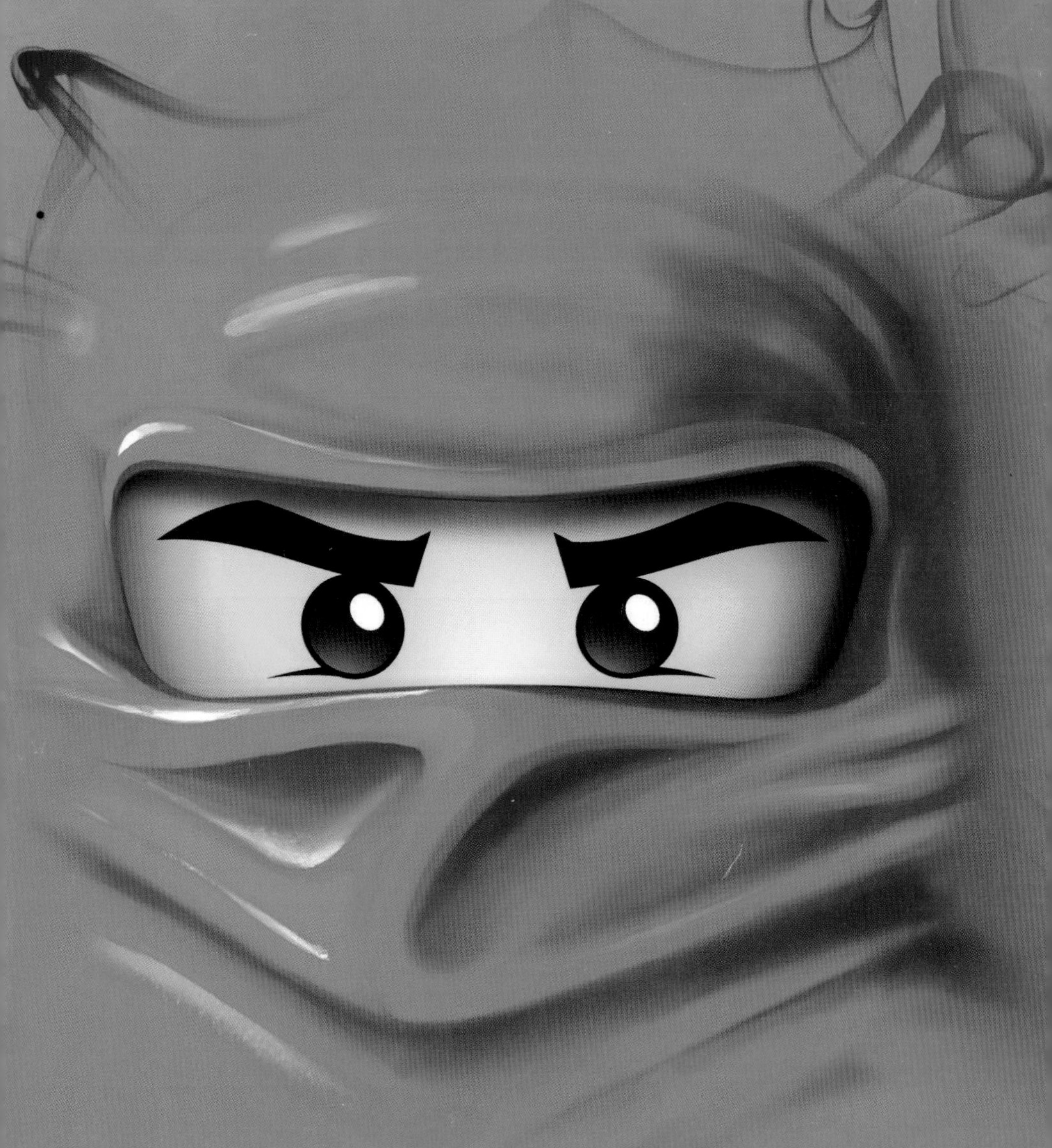

PAPERCUTZ™

LEGO® GRAPHIC NOVELS AVAILABLE FROM PAPERCUTZ™

NINJAGO #1

NINJAGO #2

NINJAGO #3

NINJAGO #4

BIONICLE #1

BIONICLE #2

BIONICLE #3

BIONICLE #4

BIONICLE #5

BIONICLE #6

BIONICLE #7

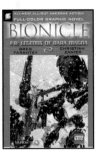

BIONICLE #8

BIONICLE #9

Mata Nui's Guide
to Bara Magna

#4 TOMB OF THE FANGPYRE

Greg Farshtey – Writer
Jolyon Yates – Artist
Jayjay Jackson – Colorist

New York

NINJAGO Masters of Spinjitzu
#4 "Tomb of the Fangpyre"

GREG FARSHTEY – Writer
JOLYON YATES – Artist
JAYJAY JACKSON – Colorist
BRYAN SENKA – Letterer

Production by NELSON DESIGN GROUP, LLC
Special thanks to ROBERTO GUEDES and STEVE DITKO
Associate Editor – MICHAEL PETRANEK
JIM SALICRUP
Editor-in-Chief

ISBN: 978-1-59707-329-5 paperback edition
ISBN: 978-1-59707-330-1 hardcover edition

Printed in US
October 2012 by Lifetouch Printing
5126 Forest Hills Ct
Loves Park, IL 61111

Distributed by Macmillan

Second Printing

MEET THE MASTERS OF SPINJITZU...

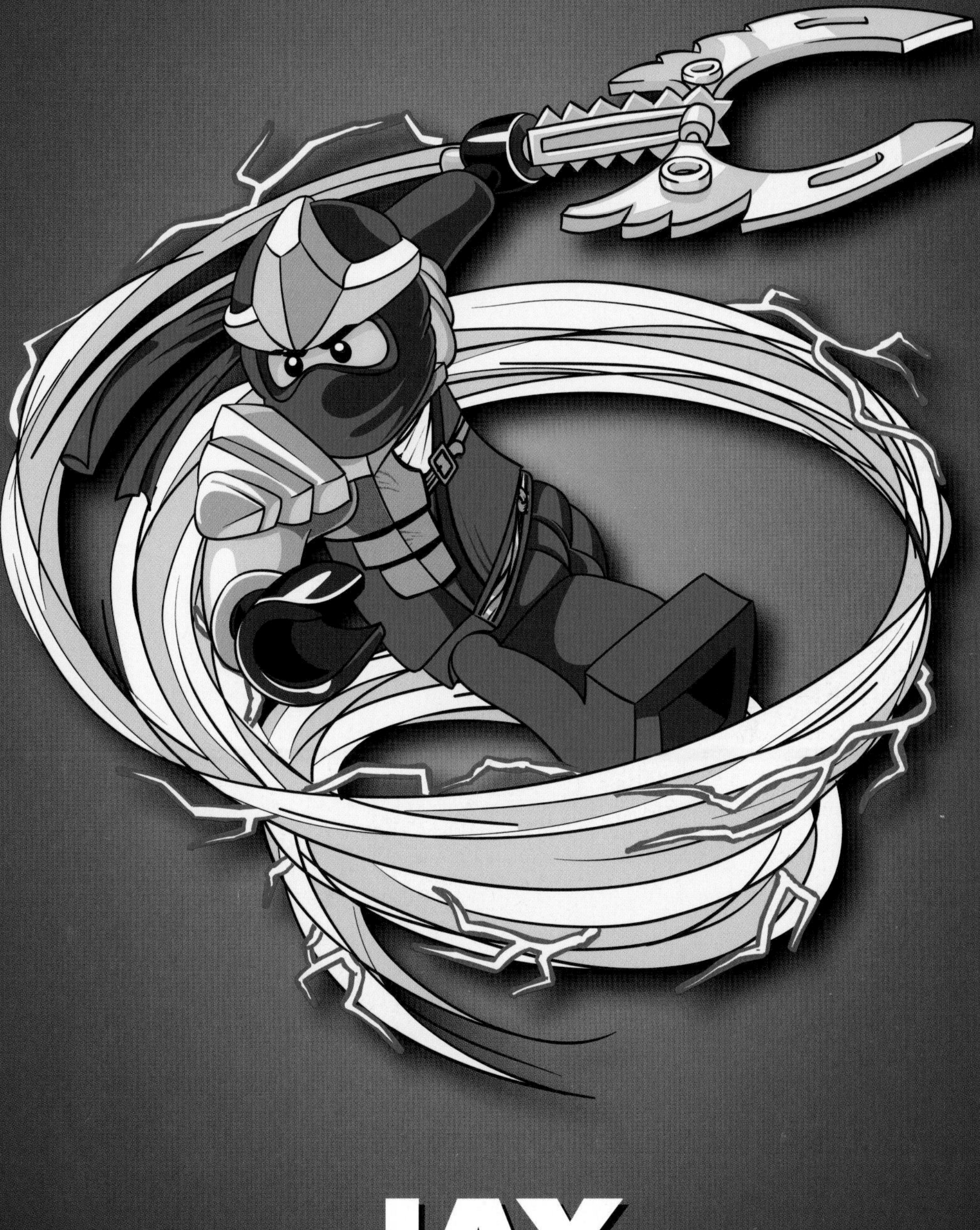

JAY

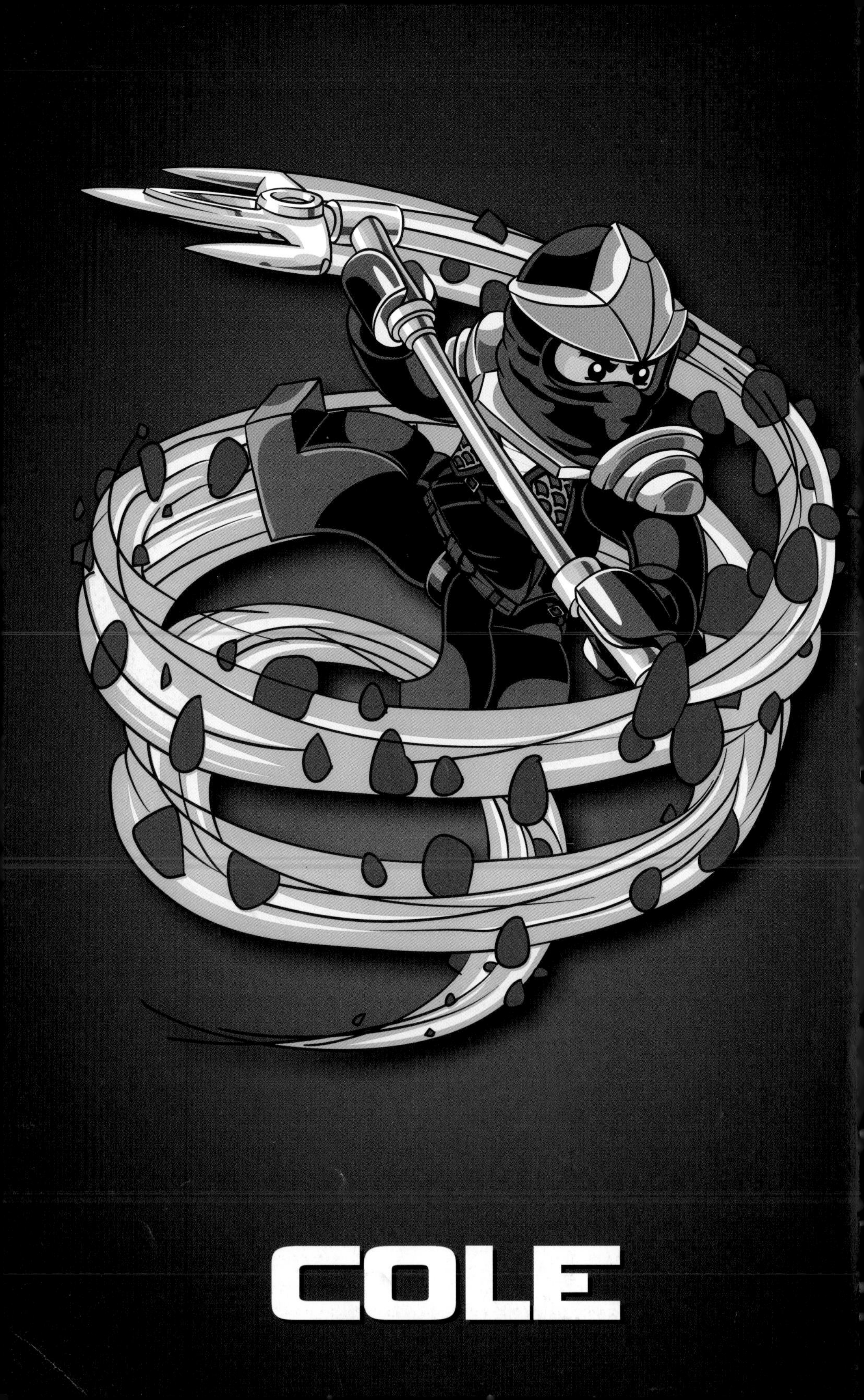

COLE

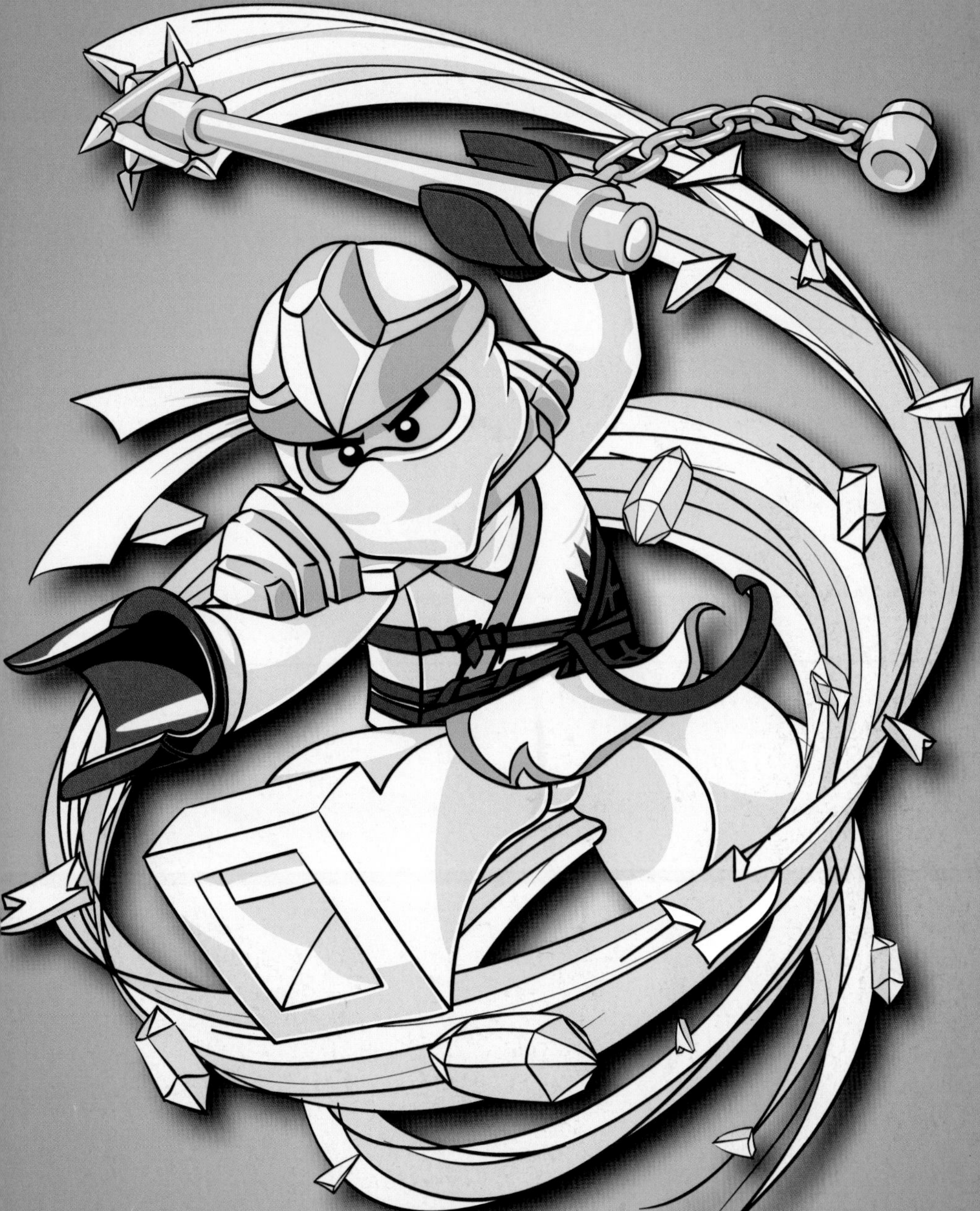

ZANE

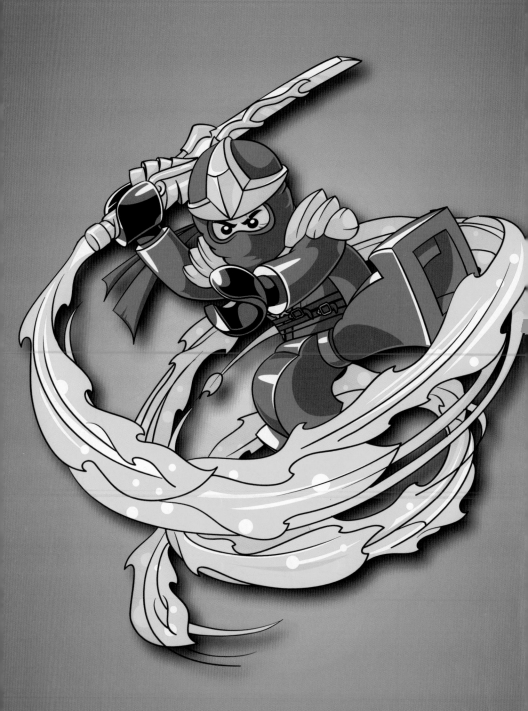

KAI

And the Master of the Masters of Spinjitzu...

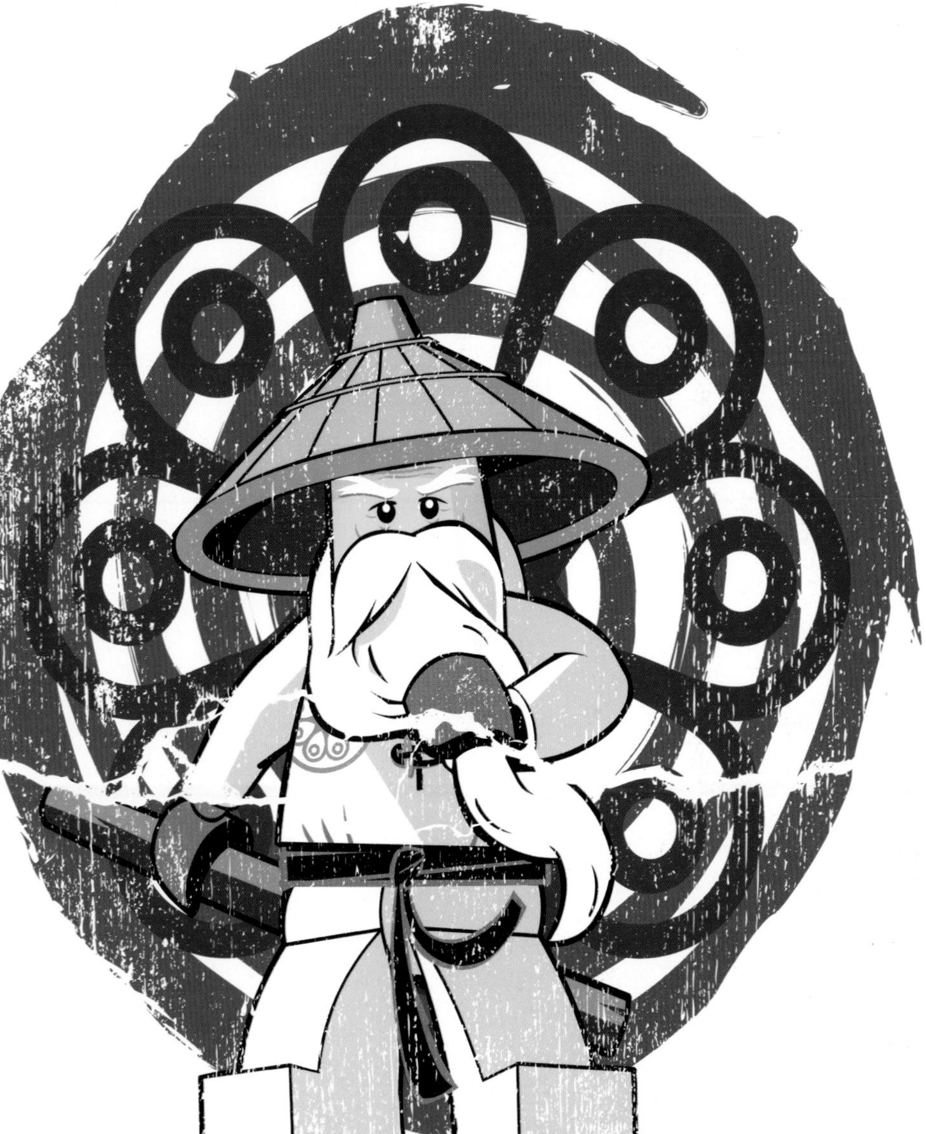

SENSEI WU

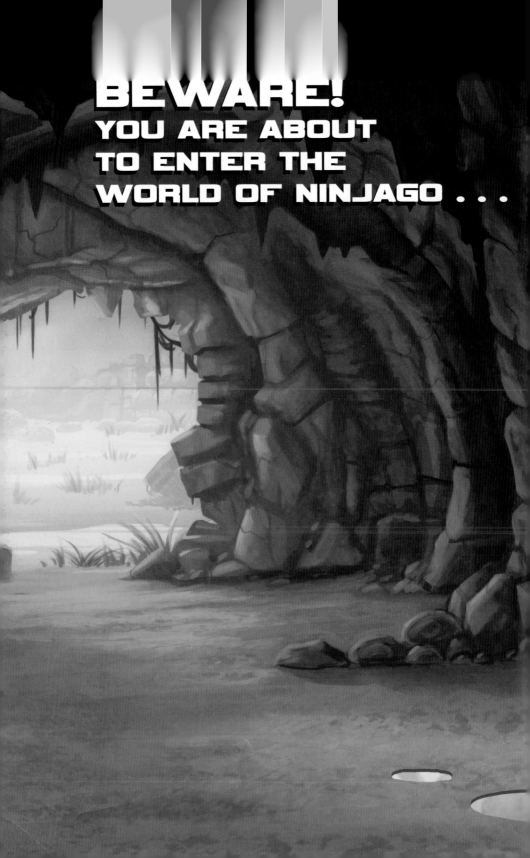

BEWARE!
YOU ARE ABOUT TO ENTER THE WORLD OF NINJAGO . . .

BEWARE!

FOR SOON YOU WILL ENTER THE TOMB OF THE FANGPYRE!

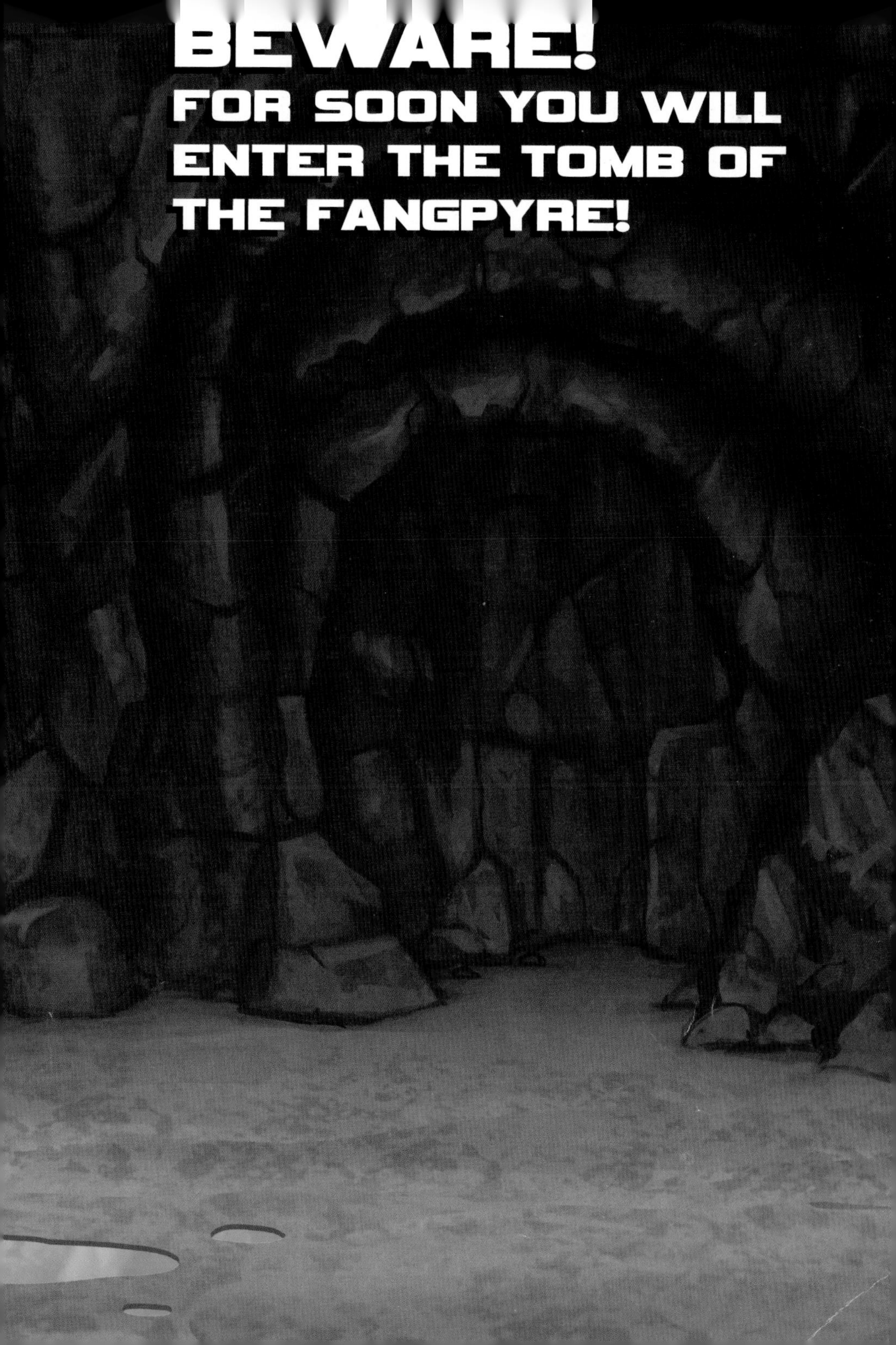

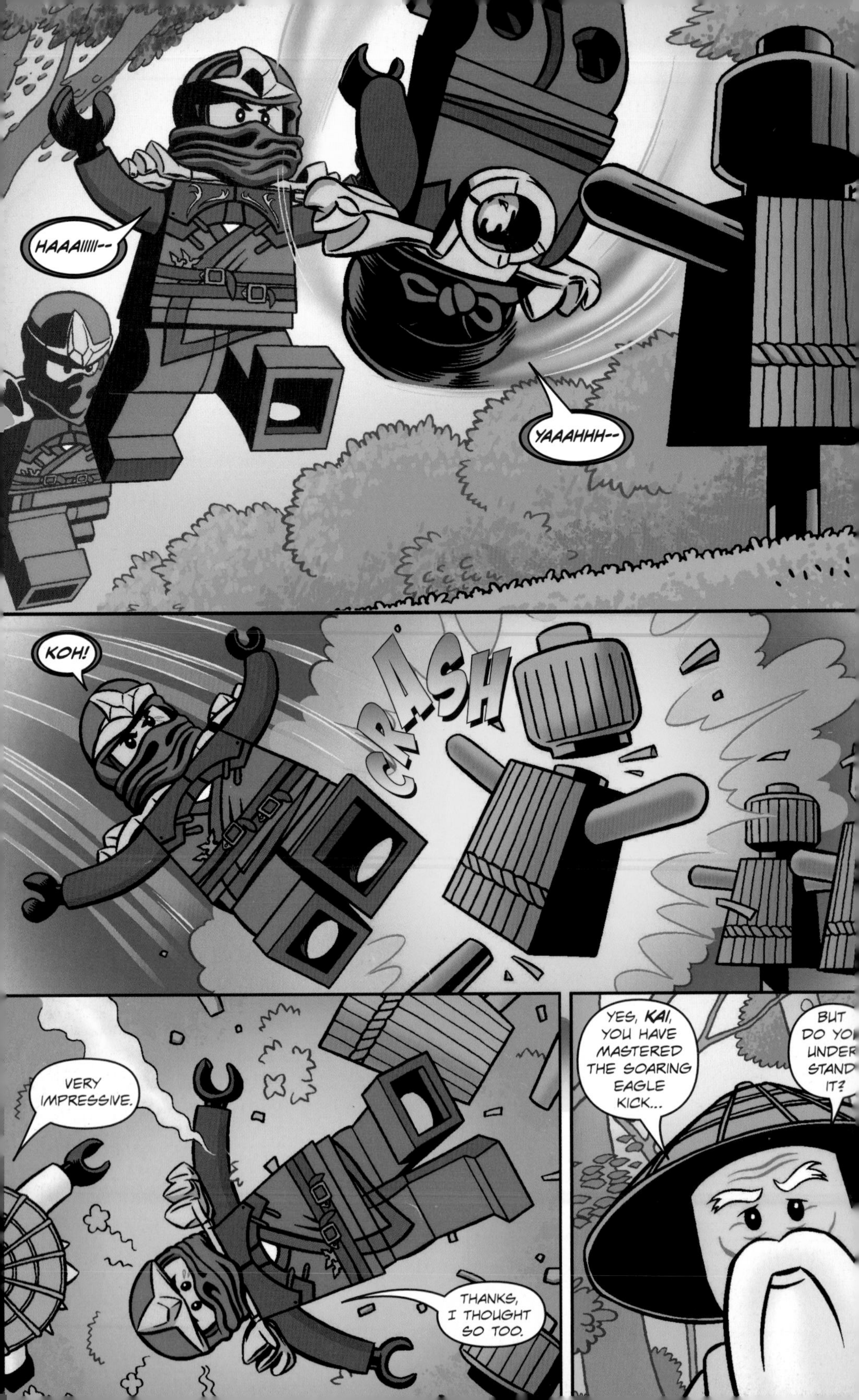
HAAAIIIII--
YAAAHHH--
KOH!
CRASH
VERY IMPRESSIVE.
THANKS, I THOUGHT SO TOO.
YES, KAI, YOU HAVE MASTERED THE SOARING EAGLE KICK...
BUT DO YO UNDER STAND IT?

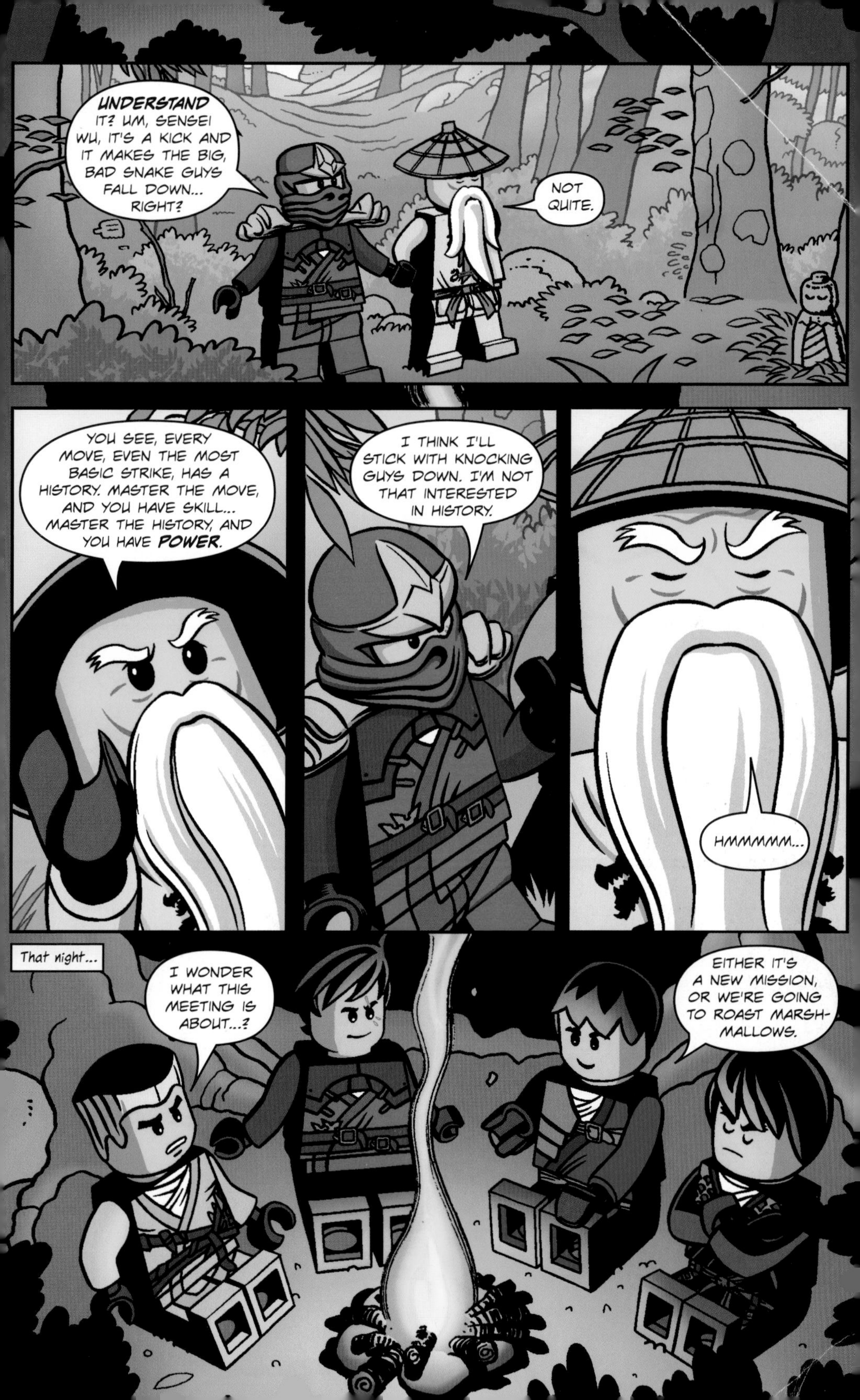
UNDERSTAND IT? UM, SENSEI WU, IT'S A KICK AND IT MAKES THE BIG, BAD SNAKE GUYS FALL DOWN... RIGHT?
NOT QUITE.
YOU SEE, EVERY MOVE, EVEN THE MOST BASIC STRIKE, HAS A HISTORY. MASTER THE MOVE, AND YOU HAVE SKILL... MASTER THE HISTORY, AND YOU HAVE POWER.
I THINK I'LL STICK WITH KNOCKING GUYS DOWN. I'M NOT THAT INTERESTED IN HISTORY.
HMMMMM...
That night...
I WONDER WHAT THIS MEETING IS ABOUT...?
EITHER IT'S A NEW MISSION, OR WE'RE GOING TO ROAST MARSH-MALLOWS.
...

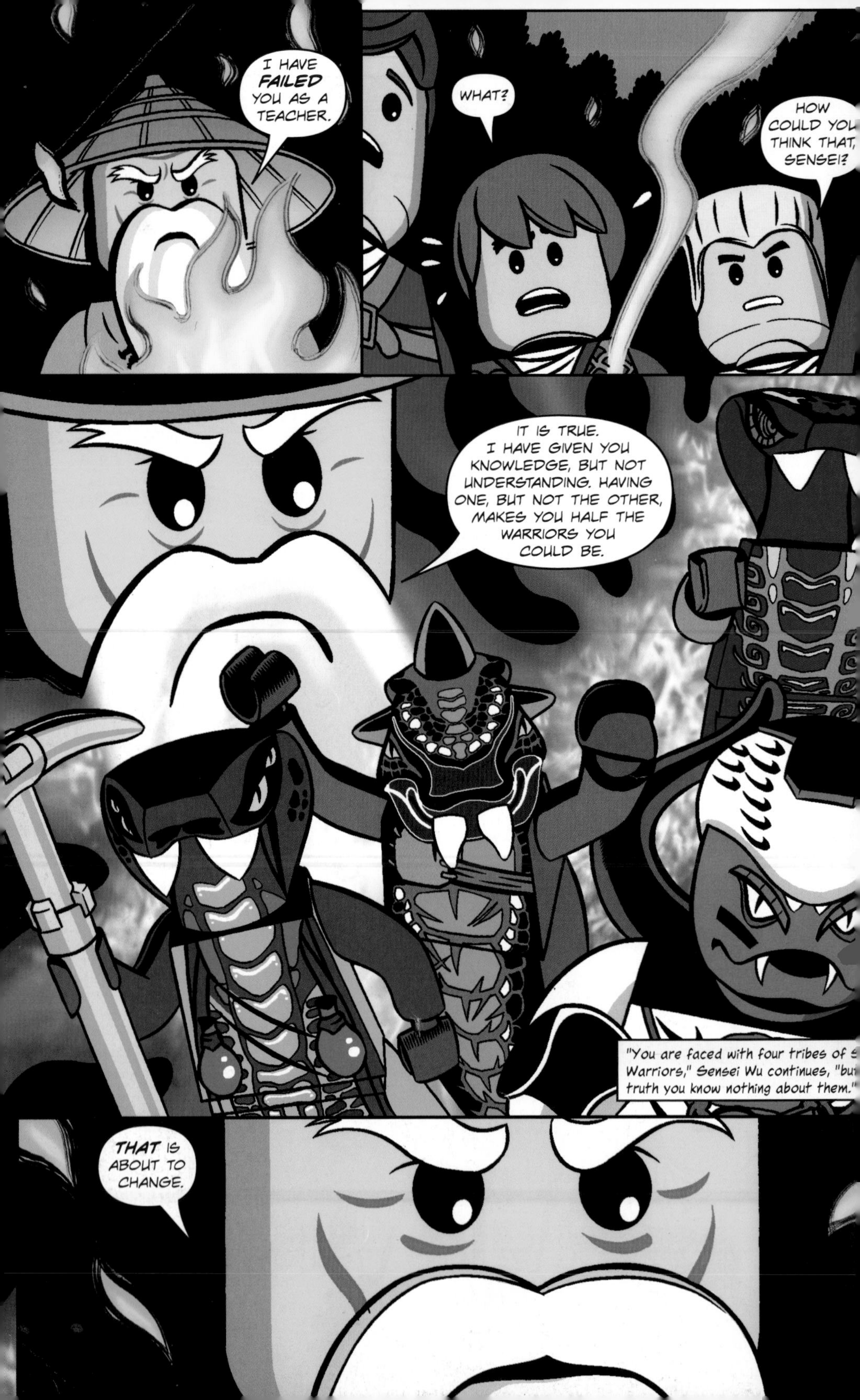
I HAVE **FAILED** YOU AS A TEACHER.
WHAT?
HOW COULD YOU THINK THAT, SENSEI?
IT IS TRUE. I HAVE GIVEN YOU KNOWLEDGE, BUT NOT UNDERSTANDING. HAVING ONE, BUT NOT THE OTHER, MAKES YOU HALF THE WARRIORS YOU COULD BE.
"You are faced with four tribes of
Warriors," Sensei Wu continues,
truth you know nothing about them."
THAT IS ABOUT TO CHANGE.

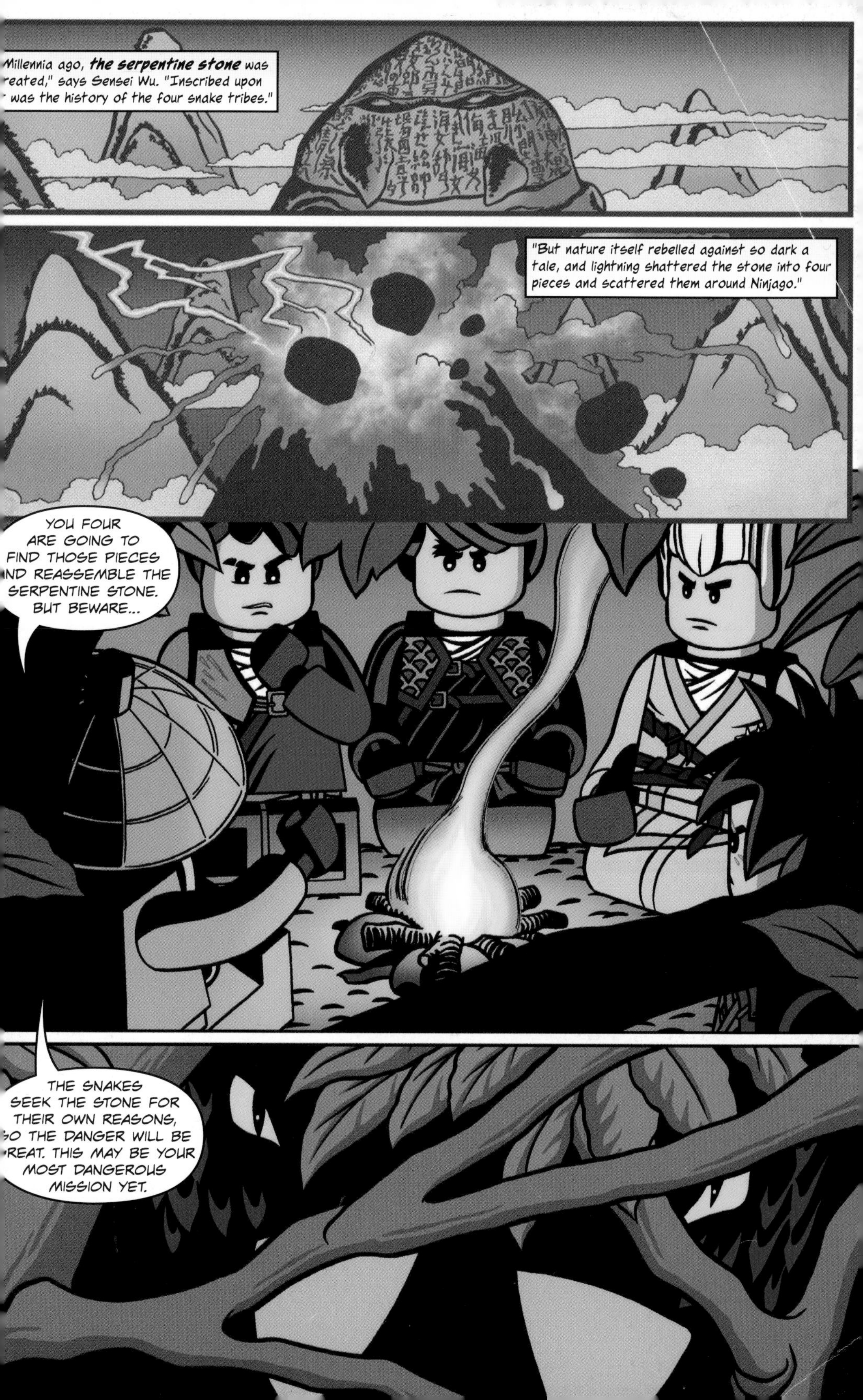

Millennia ago, **the serpentine stone** was reated," says Sensei Wu. "Inscribed upon was the history of the four snake tribes."
"But nature itself rebelled against so dark a tale, and lightning shattered the stone into four pieces and scattered them around Ninjago."
YOU FOUR ARE GOING TO FIND THOSE PIECES ND REASSEMBLE THE SERPENTINE STONE. BUT BEWARE...
THE SNAKES SEEK THE STONE FOR THEIR OWN REASONS, O THE DANGER WILL BE REAT. THIS MAY BE YOUR MOST DANGEROUS MISSION YET.

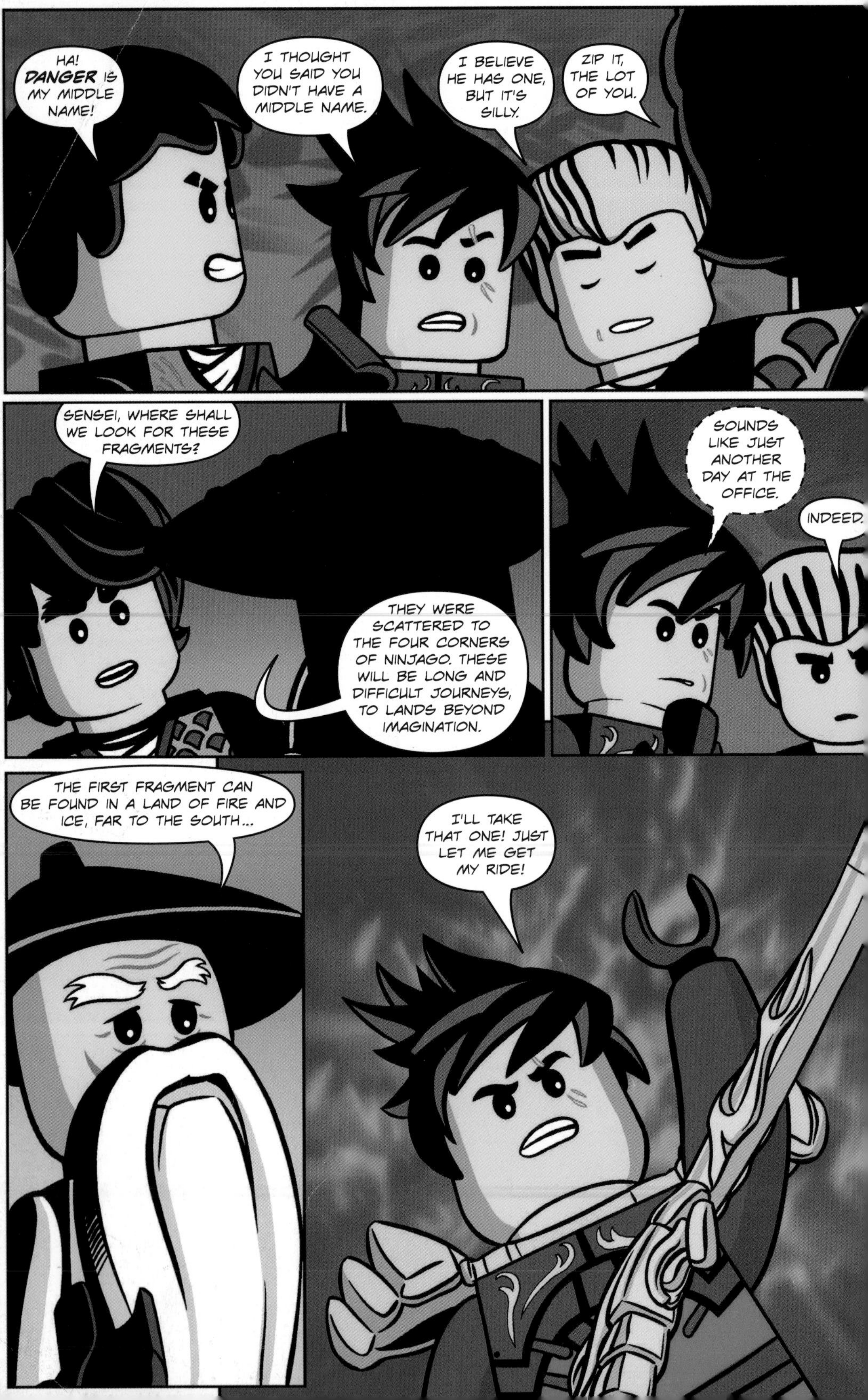
HA! DANGER IS MY MIDDLE NAME!
I THOUGHT YOU SAID YOU DIDN'T HAVE A MIDDLE NAME.
I BELIEVE HE HAS ONE, BUT IT'S SILLY.
ZIP IT, THE LOT OF YOU.
SENSEI, WHERE SHALL WE LOOK FOR THESE FRAGMENTS?
THEY WERE SCATTERED TO THE FOUR CORNERS OF NINJAGO. THESE WILL BE LONG AND DIFFICULT JOURNEYS, TO LANDS BEYOND IMAGINATION.
SOUNDS LIKE JUST ANOTHER DAY AT THE OFFICE.
INDEED.
THE FIRST FRAGMENT CAN BE FOUND IN A LAND OF FIRE AND ICE, FAR TO THE SOUTH...
I'LL TAKE THAT ONE! JUST LET ME GET MY RIDE!

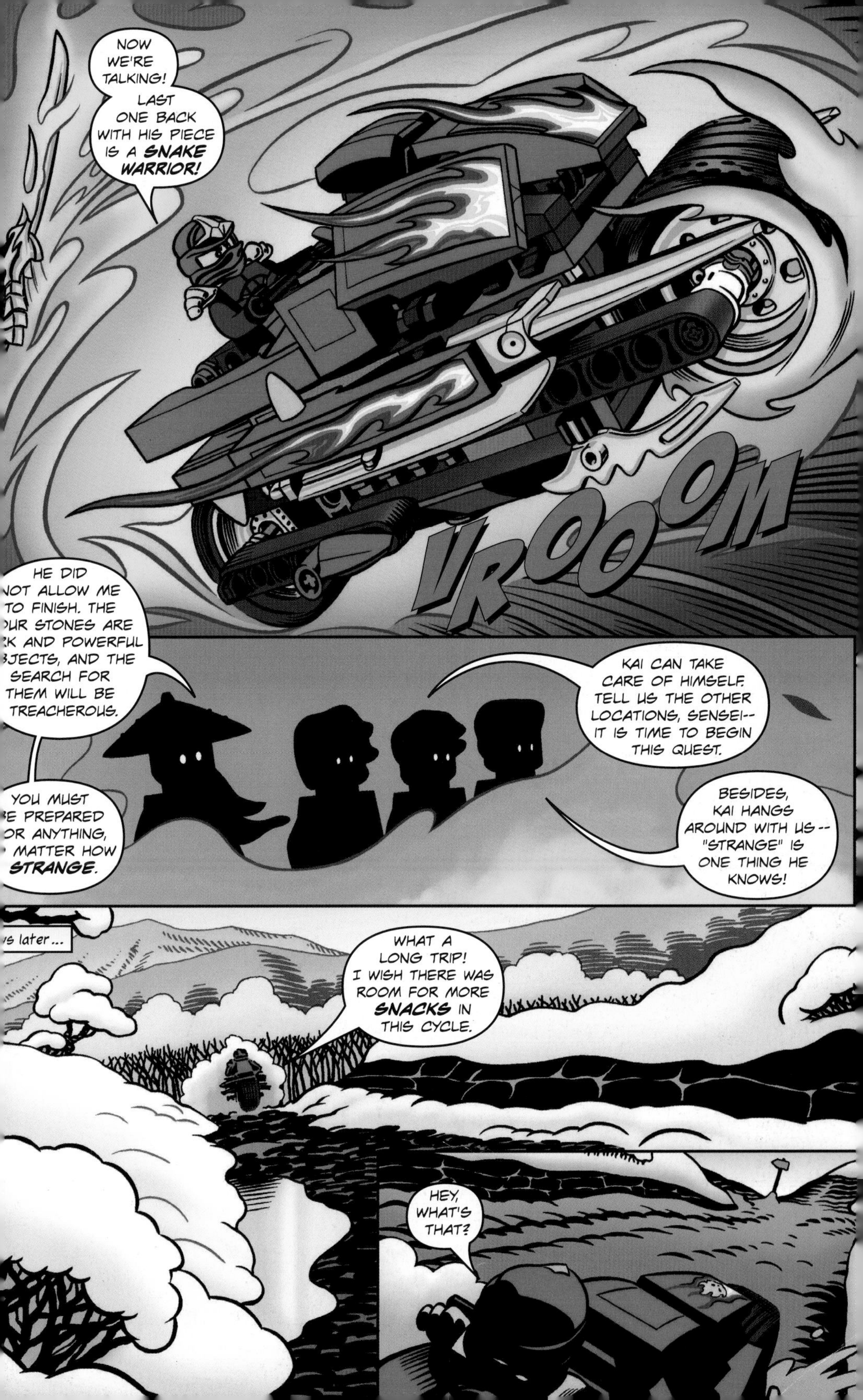
NOW WE'RE TALKING!
LAST ONE BACK WITH HIS PIECE IS A **SNAKE WARRIOR!**
VROOOOM
HE DID NOT ALLOW ME TO FINISH. THE OUR STONES ARE K AND POWERFUL BJECTS, AND THE SEARCH FOR THEM WILL BE TREACHEROUS.
YOU MUST E PREPARED OR ANYTHING, MATTER HOW **STRANGE**.
KAI CAN TAKE CARE OF HIMSELF. TELL US THE OTHER LOCATIONS, SENSEI-- IT IS TIME TO BEGIN THIS QUEST.
BESIDES, KAI HANGS AROUND WITH US -- "STRANGE" IS ONE THING HE KNOWS!
s later...
WHAT A LONG TRIP! I WISH THERE WAS ROOM FOR MORE **SNACKS** IN THIS CYCLE.
HEY, WHAT'S THAT?

THIS WAY TO SERPENTINE STONE

OH, YOU'VE GOT TO BE KIDDING...

THIS WAY TO SERPENTINE STONE

IF SOMEONE WANTS ME GOING ONE WAY, I'M GOING THE *OTHER* WAY.

Later...

NO POINT SEARCHING IN THE DARK. I'LL MAKE A FIRE AND CAMP FOR THE NIGHT.

THERE WE GO, A NICE, BLAZING--

...*PIECE OF ICE.* HUH?

YIII!

A FROZEN FIRE AND RED-HOT SNOW? WHAT KIND OF A *CRAZY* PLACE IS THIS?

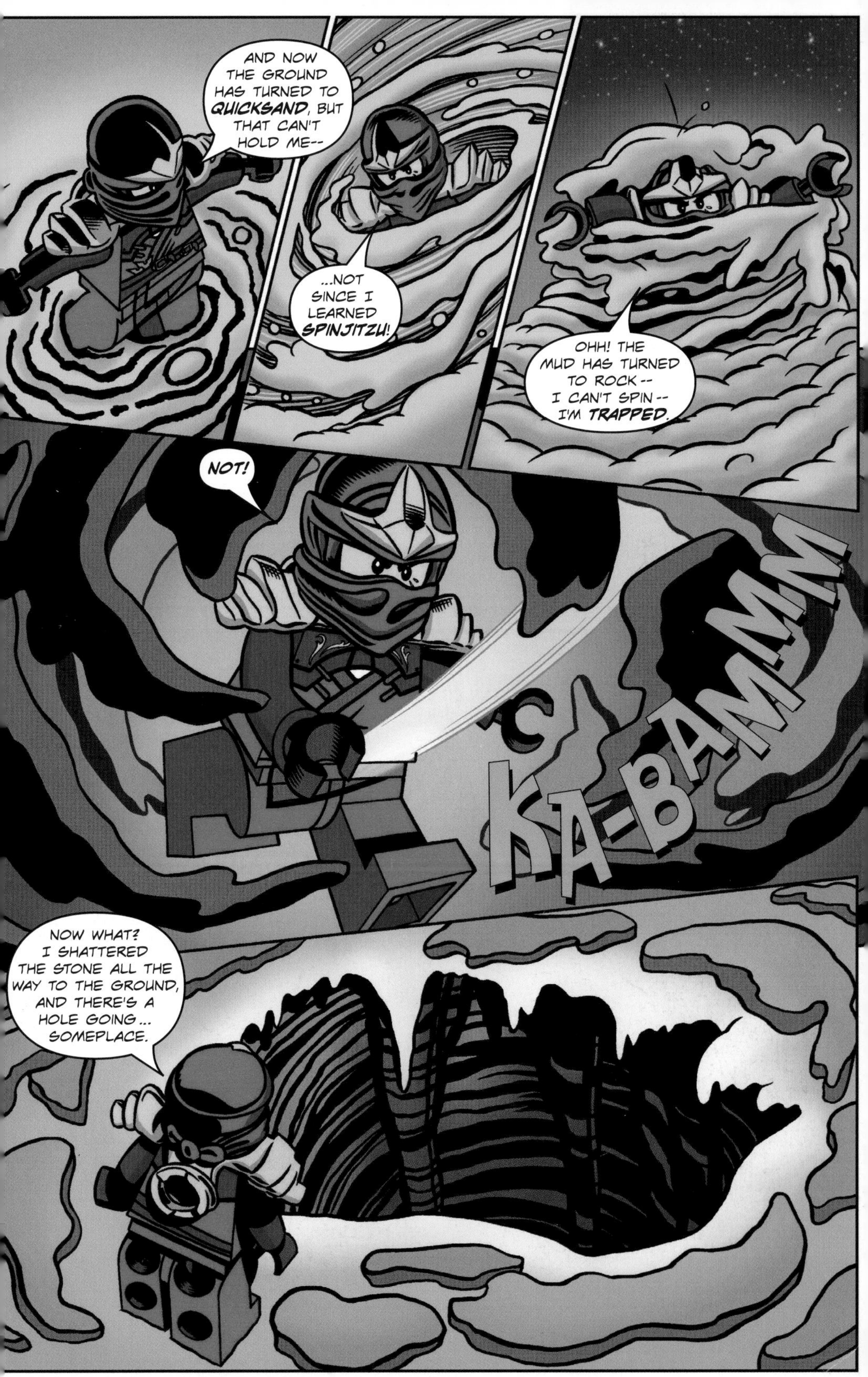
AND NOW THE GROUND HAS TURNED TO QUICKSAND, BUT THAT CAN'T HOLD ME--
...NOT SINCE I LEARNED SPINJITZU!
OHH! THE MUD HAS TURNED TO ROCK -- I CAN'T SPIN -- I'M TRAPPED.
NOT!
KA-BAMMM
NOW WHAT? I SHATTERED THE STONE ALL THE WAY TO THE GROUND, AND THERE'S A HOLE GOING... SOMEPLACE.

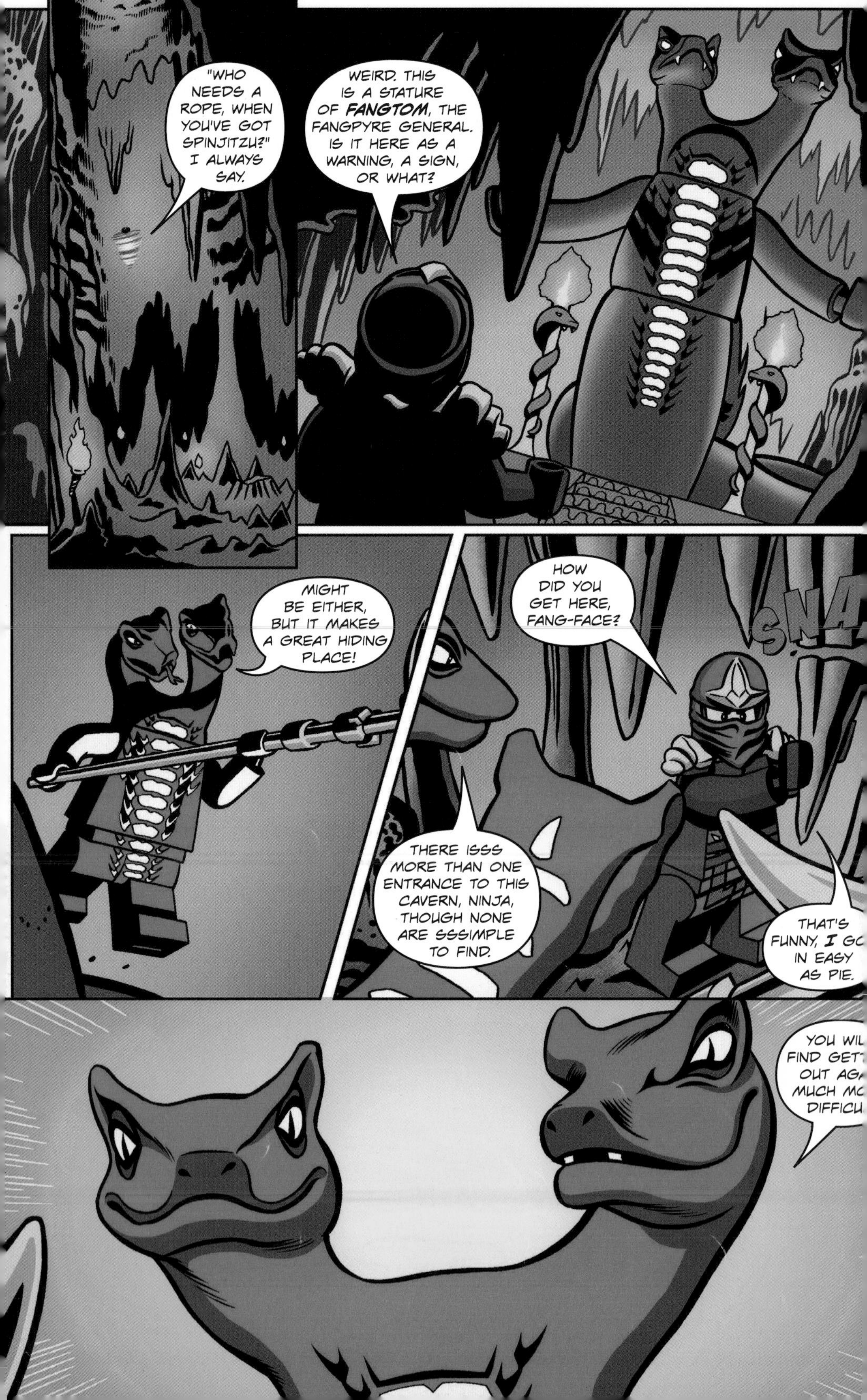

"WHO NEEDS A ROPE, WHEN YOU'VE GOT SPINJITZU?" I ALWAYS SAY.
WEIRD. THIS IS A STATURE OF **FANGTOM**, THE FANGPYRE GENERAL. IS IT HERE AS A WARNING, A SIGN, OR WHAT?
MIGHT BE EITHER, BUT IT MAKES A GREAT HIDING PLACE!
HOW DID YOU GET HERE, FANG-FACE?
SNA
THERE ISSS MORE THAN ONE ENTRANCE TO THIS CAVERN, NINJA, THOUGH NONE ARE SSSIMPLE TO FIND.
THAT'S FUNNY, **I** G IN EASY AS PIE.
YOU WIL FIND GET OUT AG MUCH MO DIFFICU

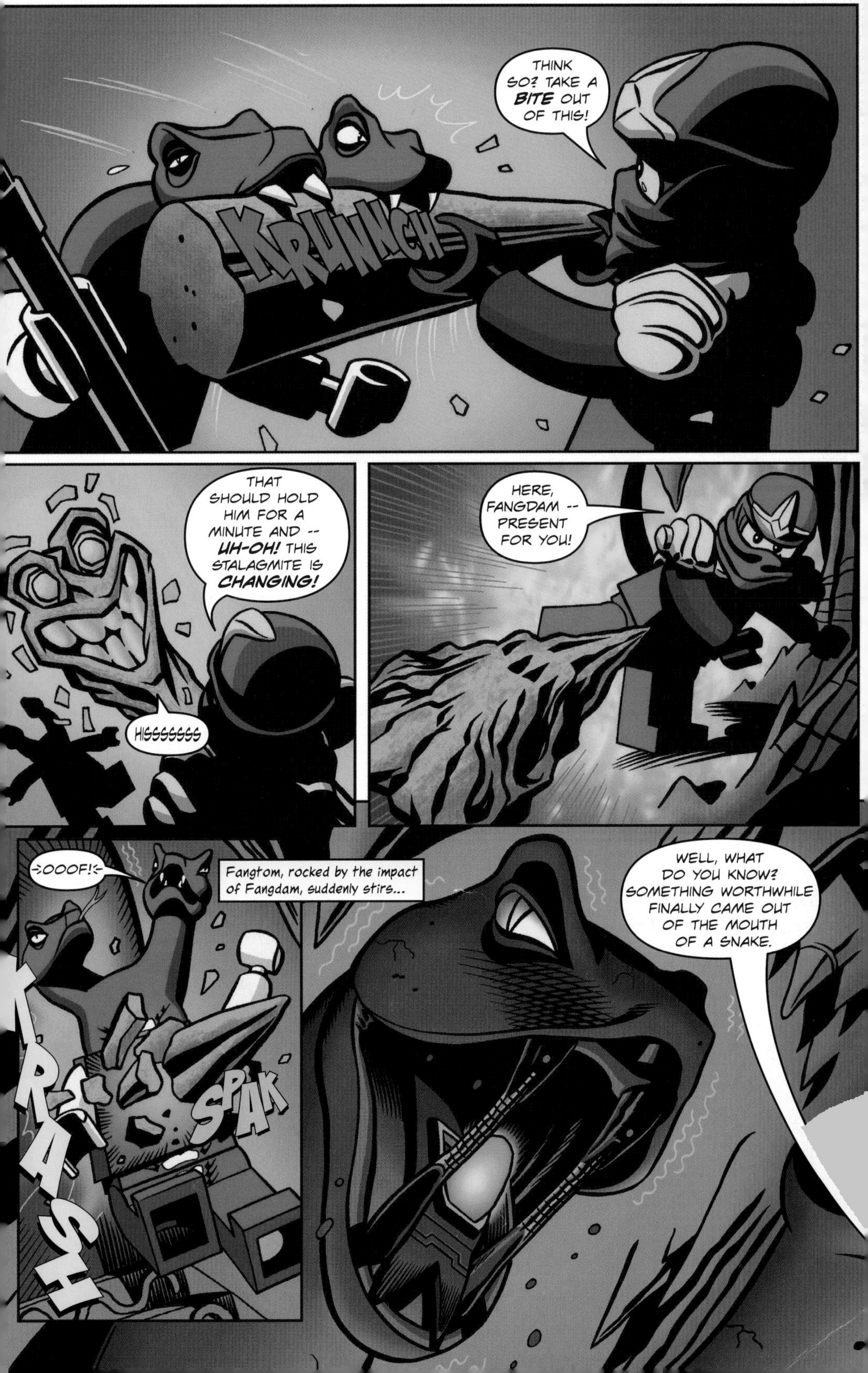
THINK SO? TAKE A BITE OUT OF THIS!
KRUNNCH
THAT SHOULD HOLD HIM FOR A MINUTE AND -- UH-OH! THIS STALAGMITE IS CHANGING!
HISSSSSSS
HERE, FANGDAM -- PRESENT FOR YOU!
OOOF!
Fangtom, rocked by the impact of Fangdam, suddenly stirs...
KRASH
SPAK
WELL, WHAT DO YOU KNOW? SOMETHING WORTHWHILE FINALLY CAME OUT OF THE MOUTH OF A SNAKE.

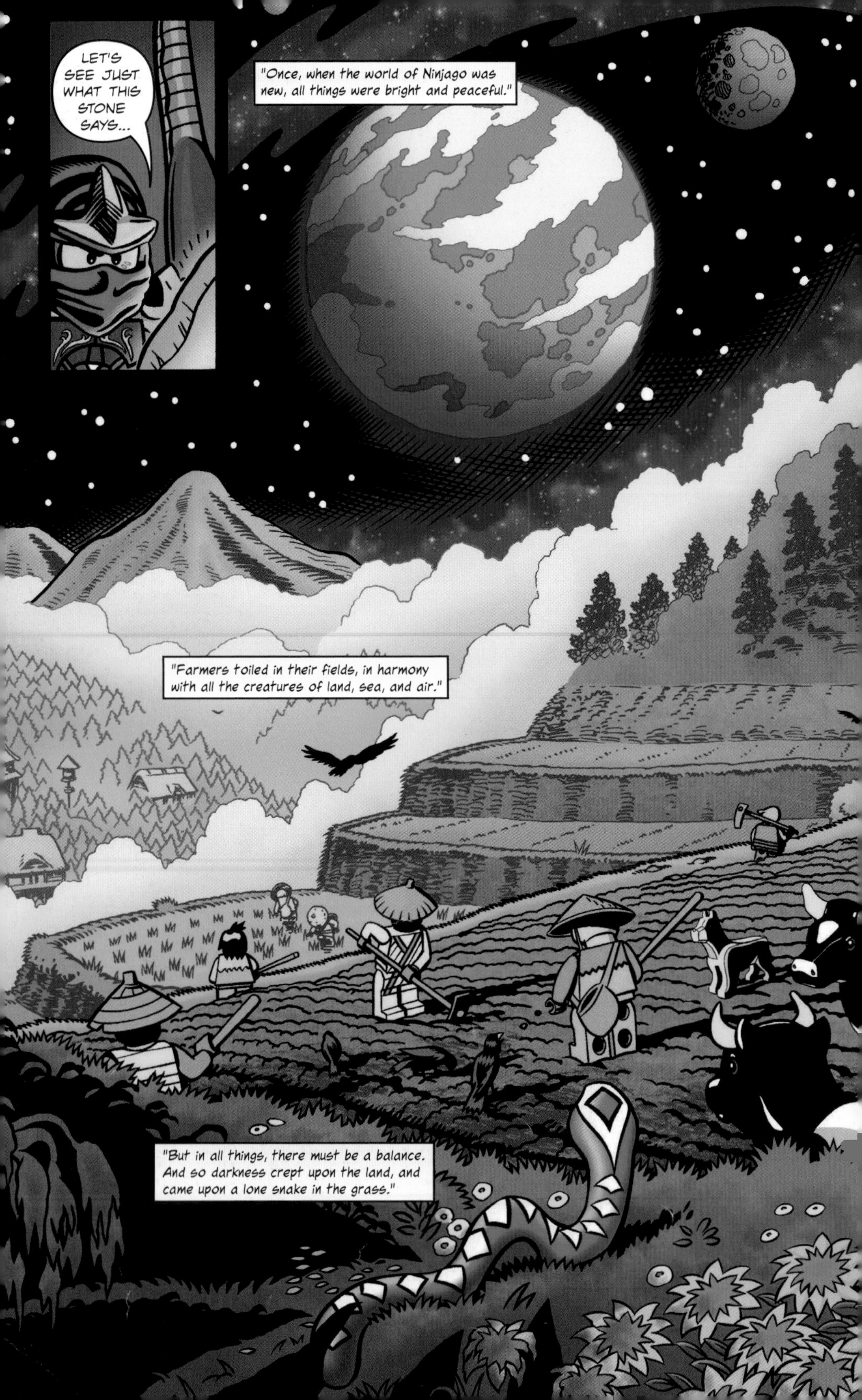
LET'S SEE JUST WHAT THIS STONE SAYS...
"Once, when the world of Ninjago was new, all things were bright and peaceful."
"Farmers toiled in their fields, in harmony with all the creatures of land, sea, and air."
"But in all things, there must be a balance. And so darkness crept upon the land, and came upon a lone snake in the grass."

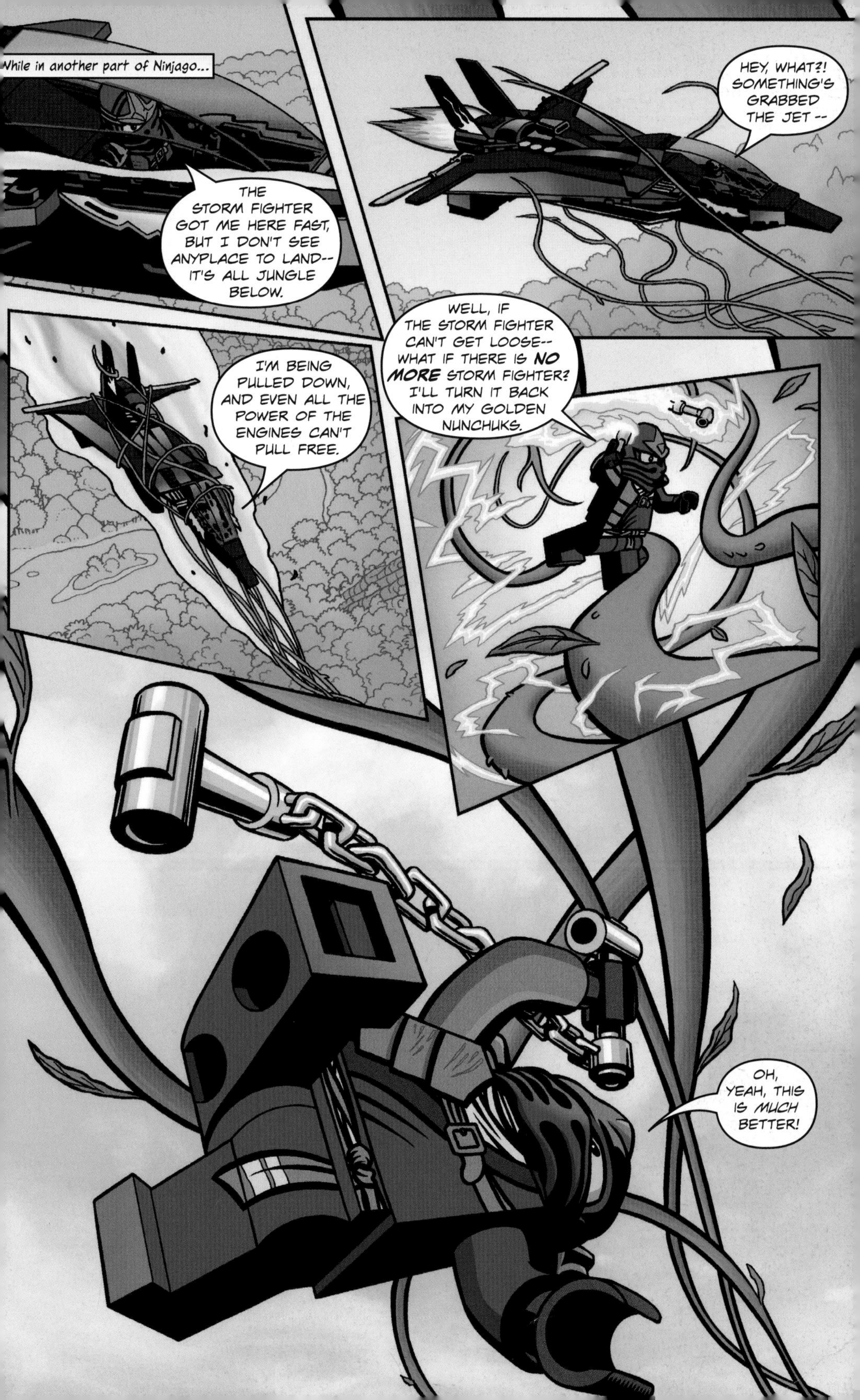
While in another part of Ninjago...
THE STORM FIGHTER GOT ME HERE FAST, BUT I DON'T SEE ANYPLACE TO LAND-- IT'S ALL JUNGLE BELOW.
HEY, WHAT?! SOMETHING'S GRABBED THE JET --
I'M BEING PULLED DOWN, AND EVEN ALL THE POWER OF THE ENGINES CAN'T PULL FREE.
WELL, IF THE STORM FIGHTER CAN'T GET LOOSE-- WHAT IF THERE IS NO MORE STORM FIGHTER? I'LL TURN IT BACK INTO MY GOLDEN NUNCHUKS.
OH, YEAH, THIS IS MUCH BETTER!

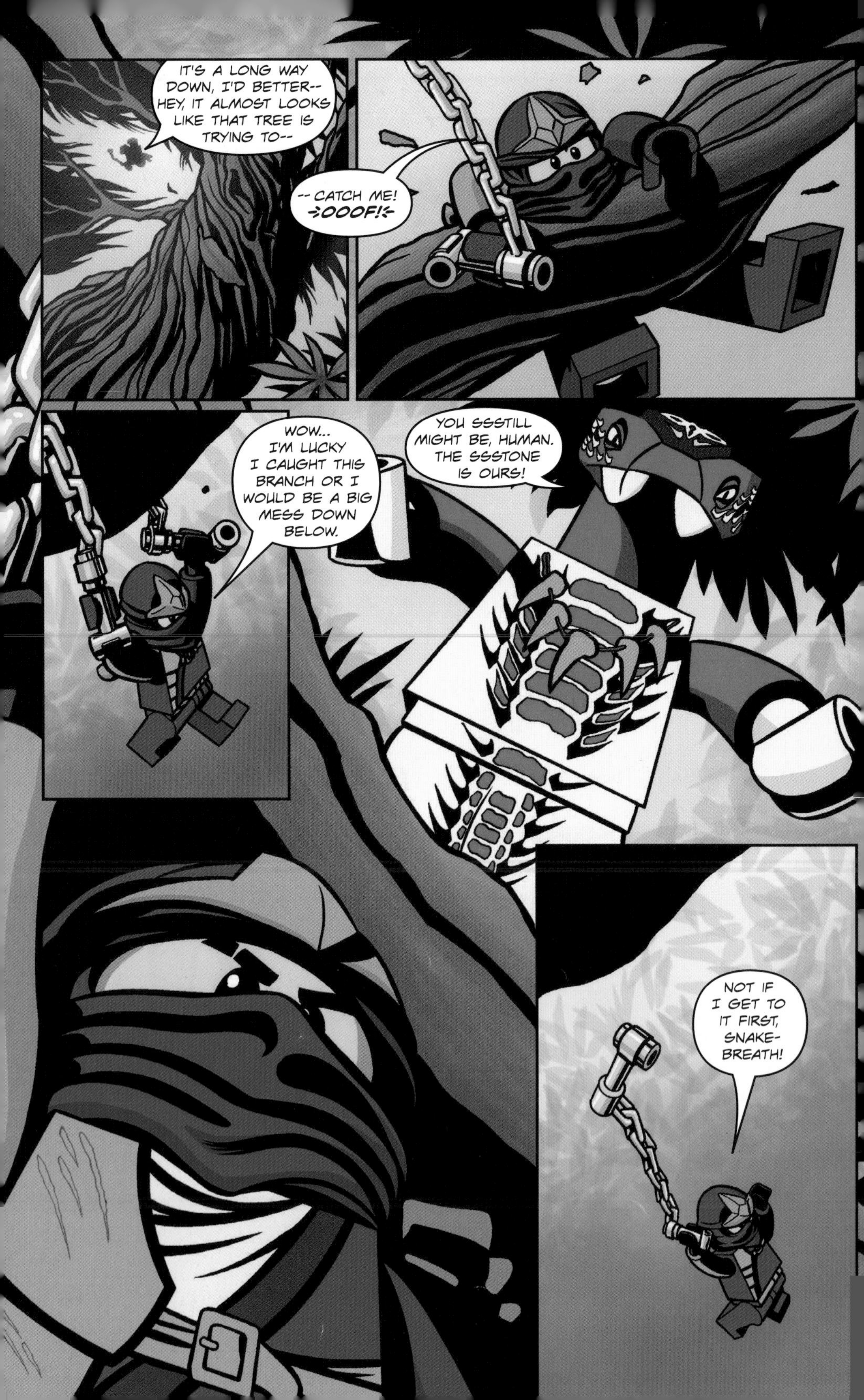

IT'S A LONG WAY DOWN, I'D BETTER-- HEY, IT ALMOST LOOKS LIKE THAT TREE IS TRYING TO--
--CATCH ME! OOOF!
WOW... I'M LUCKY I CAUGHT THIS BRANCH OR I WOULD BE A BIG MESS DOWN BELOW.
YOU SSSTILL MIGHT BE, HUMAN. THE SSSTONE IS OURS!
NOT IF I GET TO IT FIRST, SNAKE-BREATH!

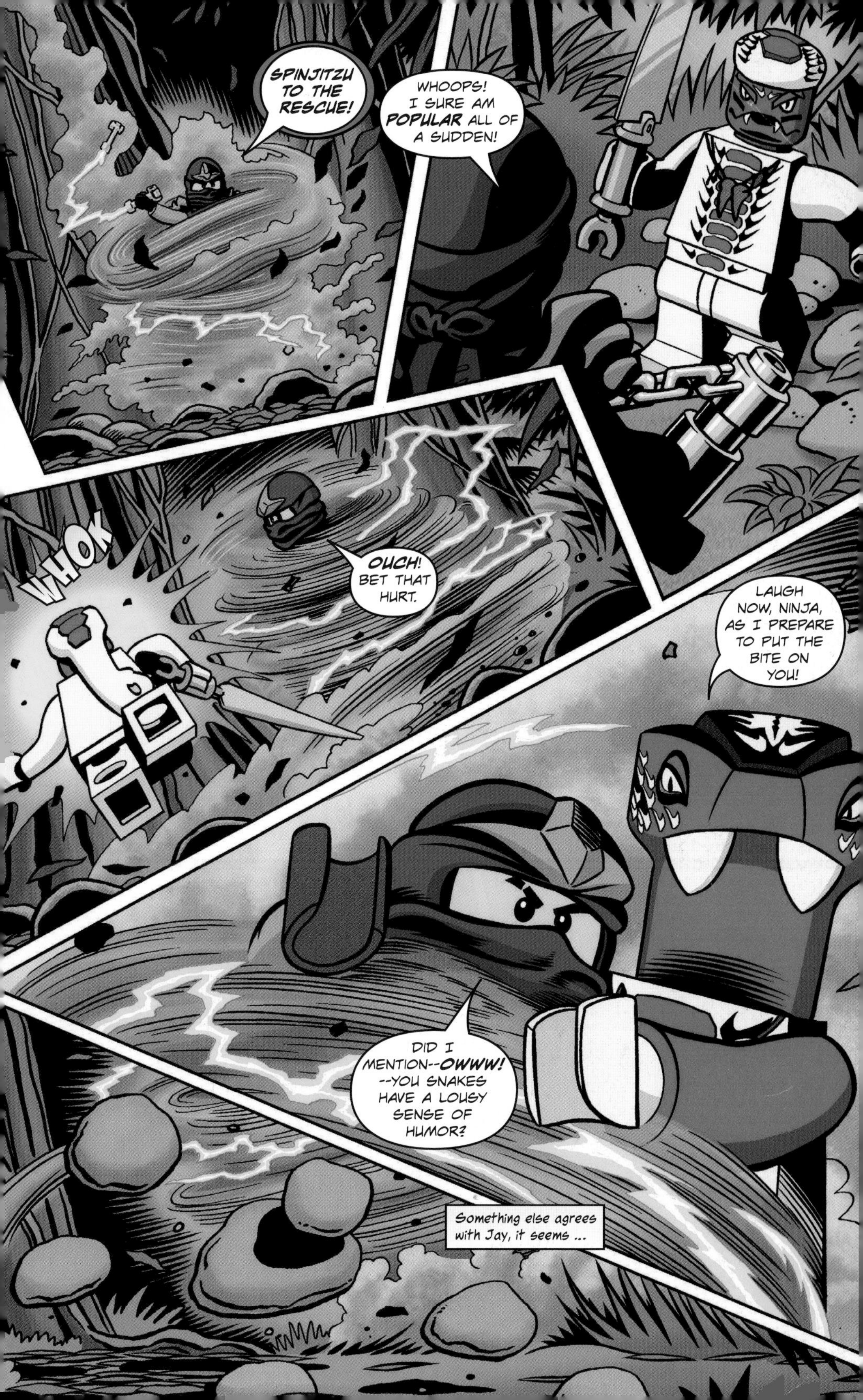
SPINJITZU TO THE RESCUE!
WHOOPS! I SURE AM POPULAR ALL OF A SUDDEN!
WHOK
OUCH! BET THAT HURT.
LAUGH NOW, NINJA, AS I PREPARE TO PUT THE BITE ON YOU!
DID I MENTION--OWWW! --YOU SNAKES HAVE A LOUSY SENSE OF HUMOR?
Something else agrees with Jay, it seems ...

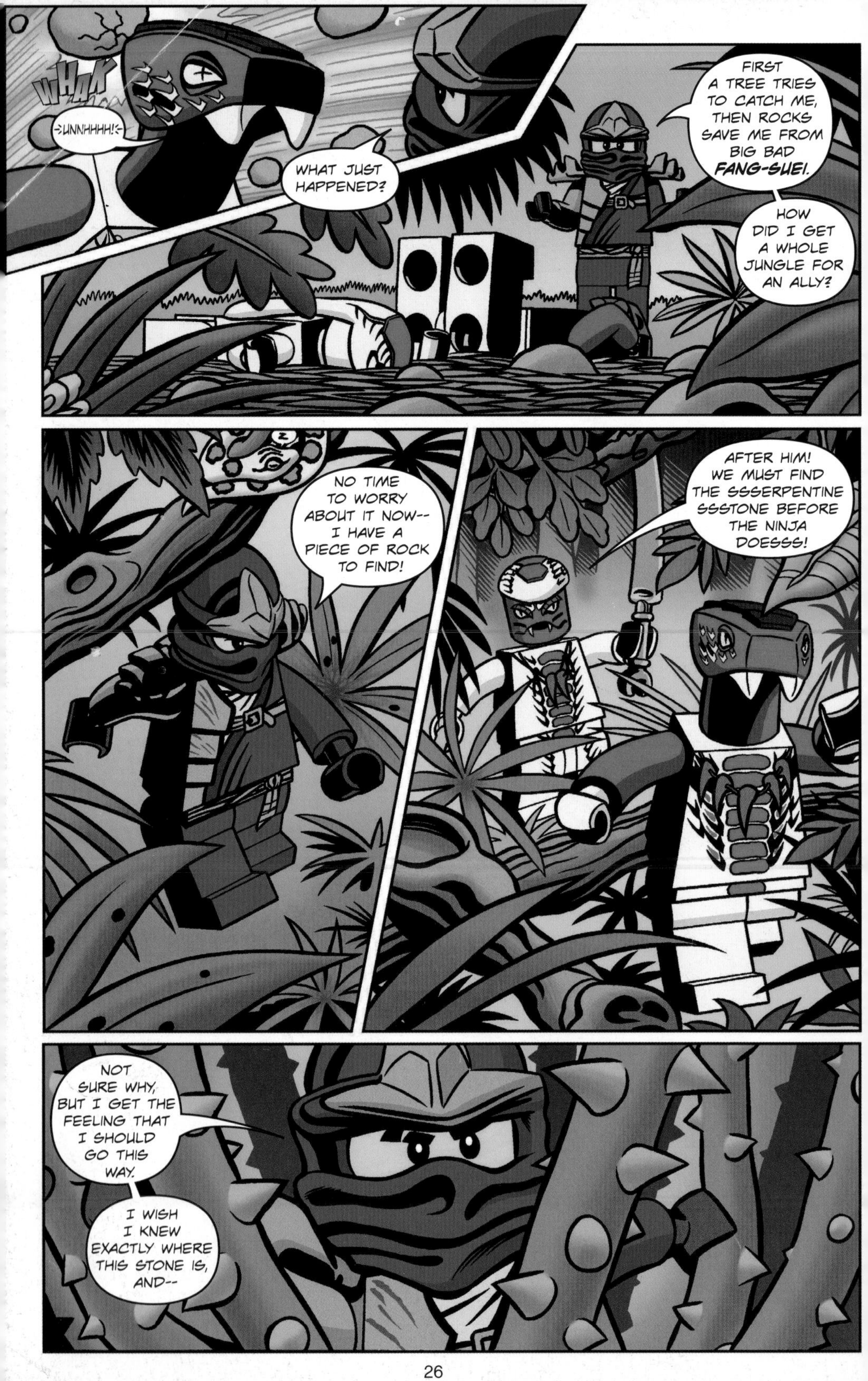
WHAK
UNNHHHH!
WHAT JUST HAPPENED?
FIRST A TREE TRIES TO CATCH ME, THEN ROCKS SAVE ME FROM BIG BAD FANG-SUEI.
HOW DID I GET A WHOLE JUNGLE FOR AN ALLY?
NO TIME TO WORRY ABOUT IT NOW-- I HAVE A PIECE OF ROCK TO FIND!
AFTER HIM! WE MUST FIND THE SSSERPENTINE SSSTONE BEFORE THE NINJA DOESSS!
NOT SURE WHY, BUT I GET THE FEELING THAT I SHOULD GO THIS WAY.
I WISH I KNEW EXACTLY WHERE THIS STONE IS, AND--

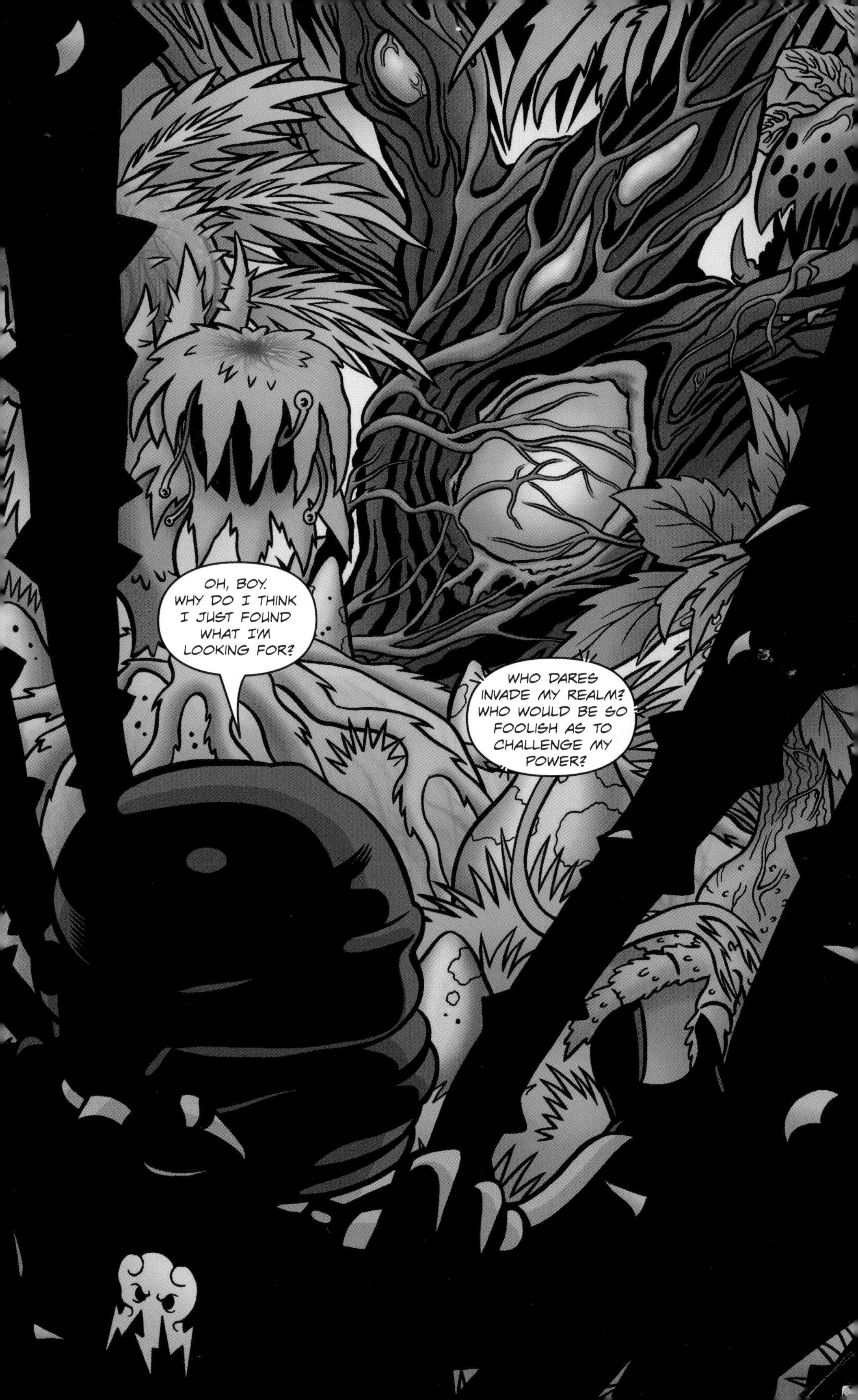
OH, BOY. WHY DO I THINK I JUST FOUND WHAT I'M LOOKING FOR?
WHO DARES INVADE MY REALM? WHO WOULD BE SO FOOLISH AS TO CHALLENGE MY POWER?

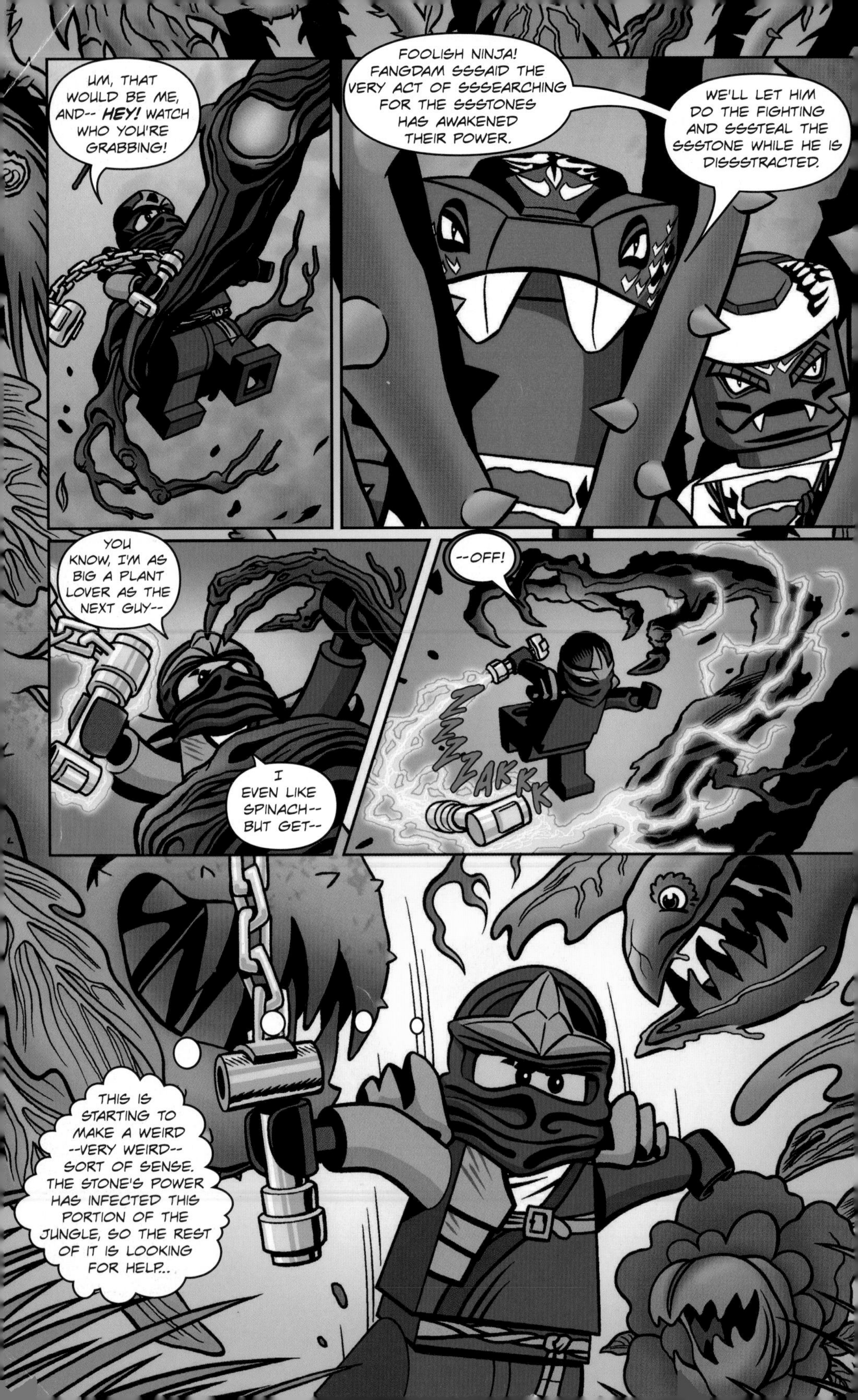
UM, THAT WOULD BE ME, AND-- **HEY!** WATCH WHO YOU'RE GRABBING!
FOOLISH NINJA! FANGDAM SSSAID THE VERY ACT OF SSSEARCHING FOR THE SSSTONES HAS AWAKENED THEIR POWER.
WE'LL LET HIM DO THE FIGHTING AND SSSTEAL THE SSSTONE WHILE HE IS DISSSTRACTED.
YOU KNOW, I'M AS BIG A PLANT LOVER AS THE NEXT GUY--
I EVEN LIKE SPINACH-- BUT GET--
--OFF!
ZZZZAKKKK
THIS IS STARTING TO MAKE A WEIRD --VERY WEIRD-- SORT OF SENSE. THE STONE'S POWER HAS INFECTED THIS PORTION OF THE JUNGLE, SO THE REST OF IT IS LOOKING FOR HELP...

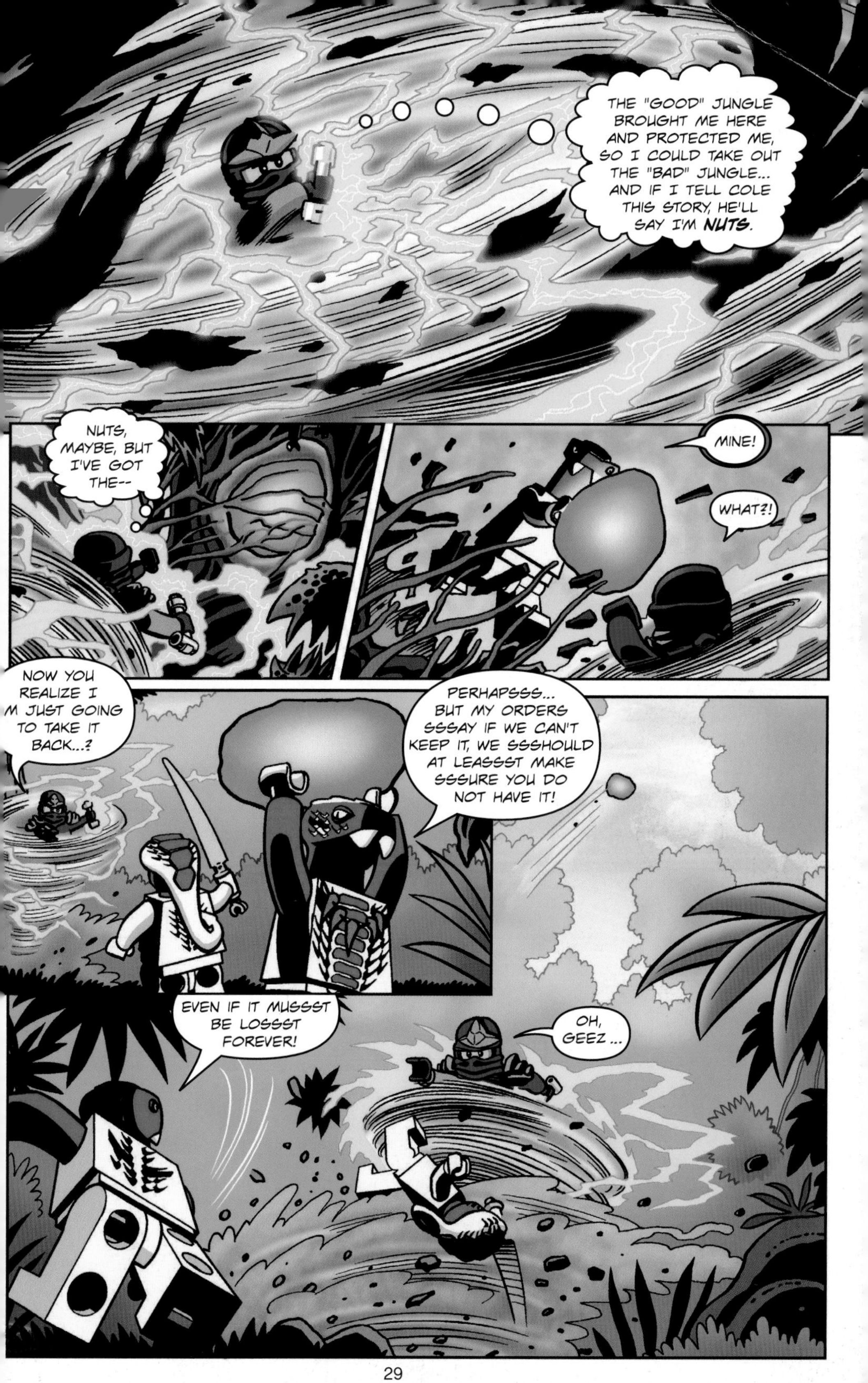

THE "GOOD" JUNGLE BROUGHT ME HERE AND PROTECTED ME, SO I COULD TAKE OUT THE "BAD" JUNGLE... AND IF I TELL COLE THIS STORY, HE'LL SAY I'M NUTS.
NUTS, MAYBE, BUT I'VE GOT THE--
MINE!
WHAT?!
NOW YOU REALIZE I M JUST GOING TO TAKE IT BACK...?
PERHAPSSS... BUT MY ORDERS SSSAY IF WE CAN'T KEEP IT, WE SSSHOULD AT LEASSST MAKE SSSURE YOU DO NOT HAVE IT!
EVEN IF IT MUSSST BE LOSSST FOREVER!
OH, GEEZ ...

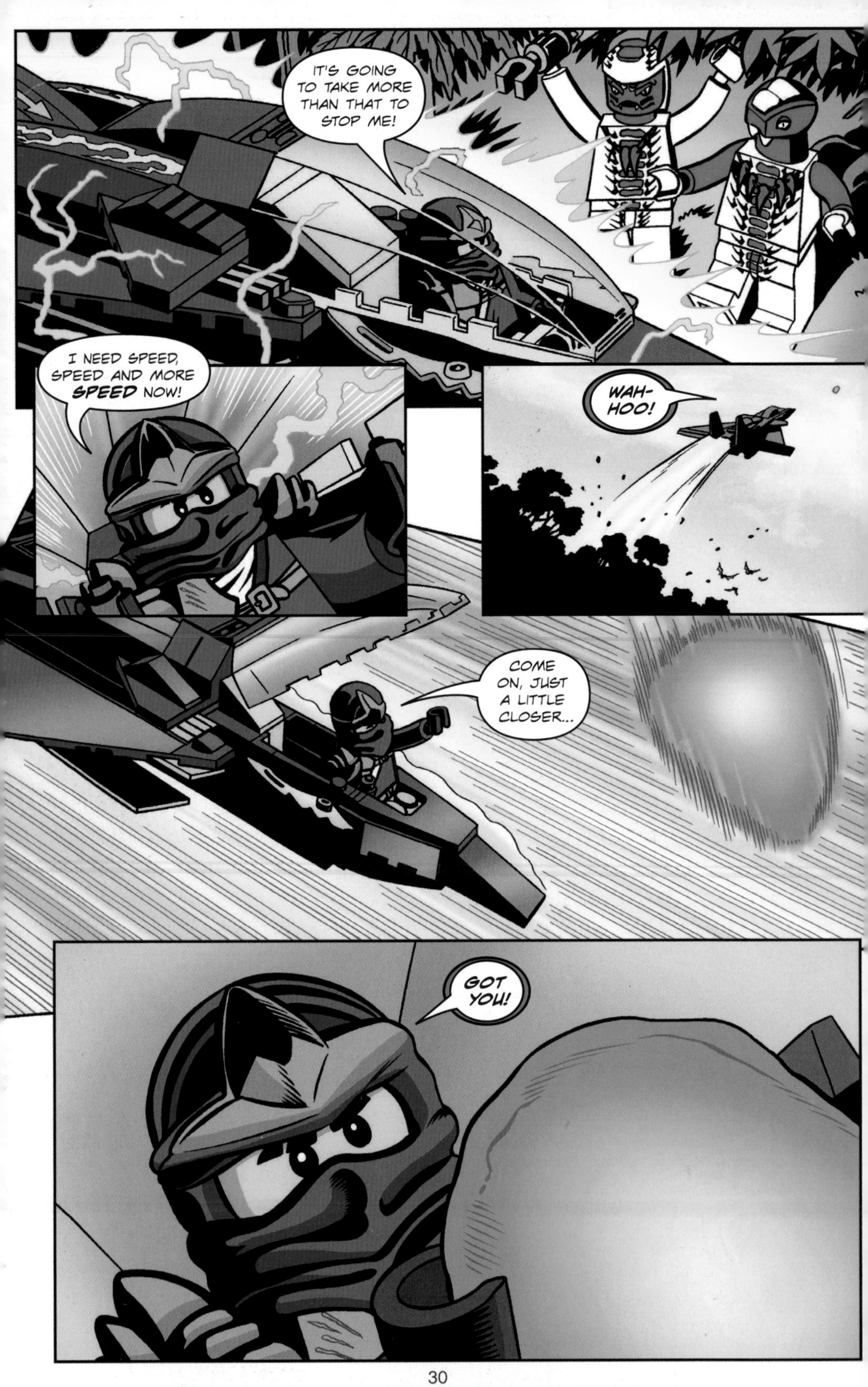
IT'S GOING TO TAKE MORE THAN THAT TO STOP ME!
I NEED SPEED, SPEED AND MORE SPEED NOW!
WAH-HOO!
COME ON, JUST A LITTLE CLOSER...
GOT YOU!

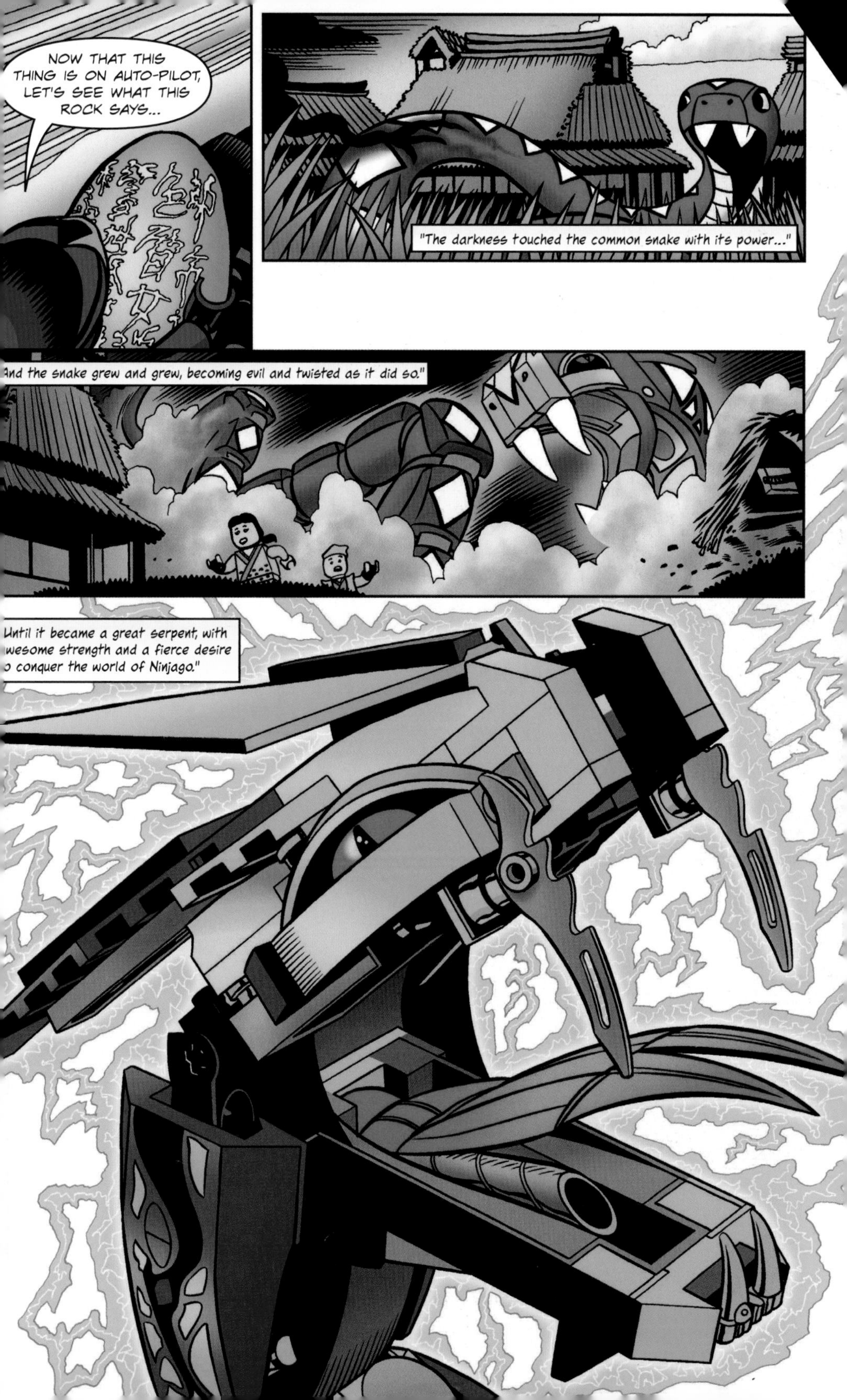
NOW THAT THIS THING IS ON AUTO-PILOT, LET'S SEE WHAT THIS ROCK SAYS...
"The darkness touched the common snake with its power..."
"And the snake grew and grew, becoming evil and twisted as it did so."
"Until it became a great serpent, with
wesome strength and a fierce desire
o conquer the world of Ninjago."

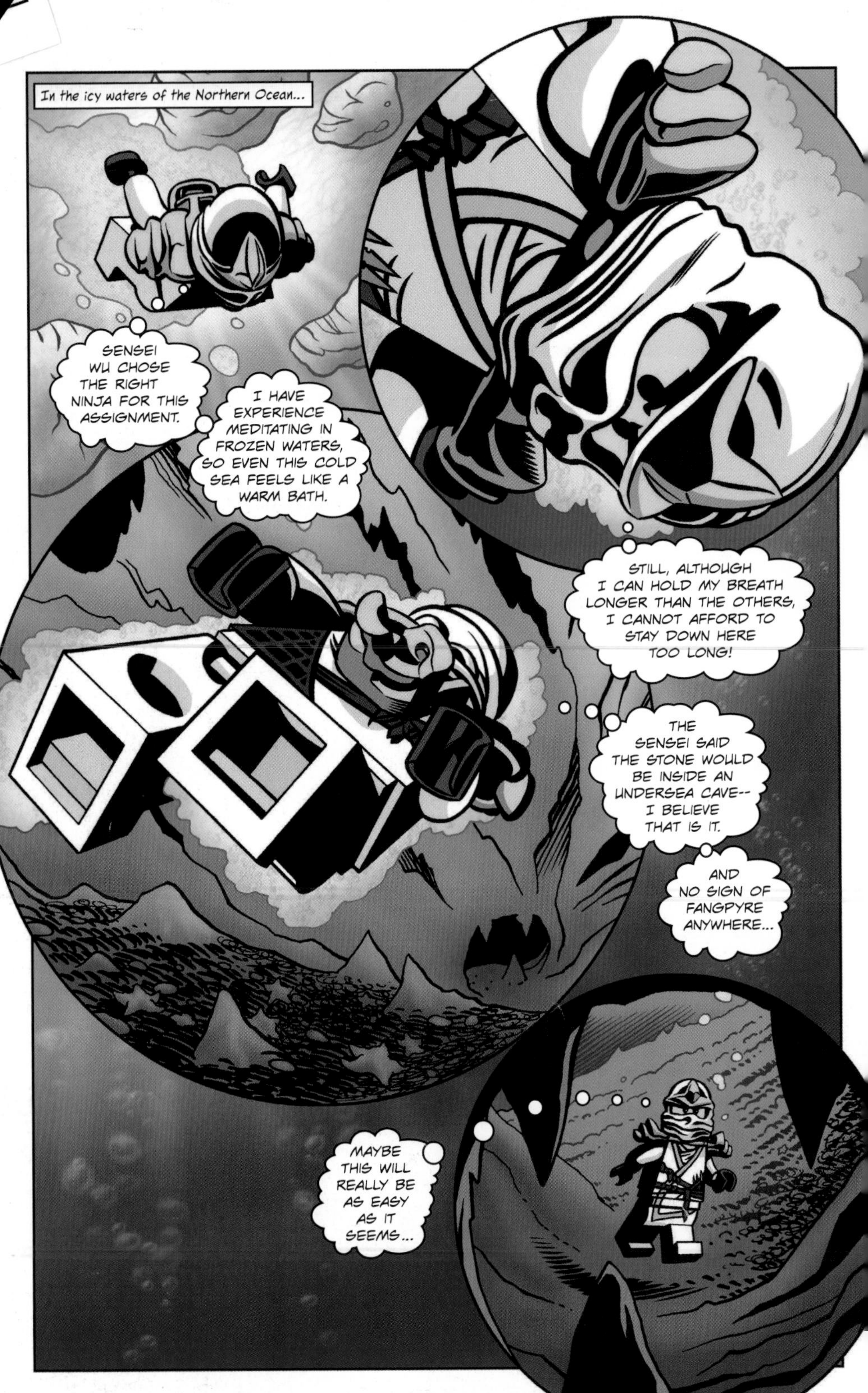
In the icy waters of the Northern Ocean...
SENSEI WU CHOSE THE RIGHT NINJA FOR THIS ASSIGNMENT.
I HAVE EXPERIENCE MEDITATING IN FROZEN WATERS, SO EVEN THIS COLD SEA FEELS LIKE A WARM BATH.
STILL, ALTHOUGH I CAN HOLD MY BREATH LONGER THAN THE OTHERS, I CANNOT AFFORD TO STAY DOWN HERE TOO LONG!
THE SENSEI SAID THE STONE WOULD BE INSIDE AN UNDERSEA CAVE-- I BELIEVE THAT IS IT.
AND NO SIGN OF FANGPYRE ANYWHERE...
MAYBE THIS WILL REALLY BE AS EASY AS IT SEEMS...

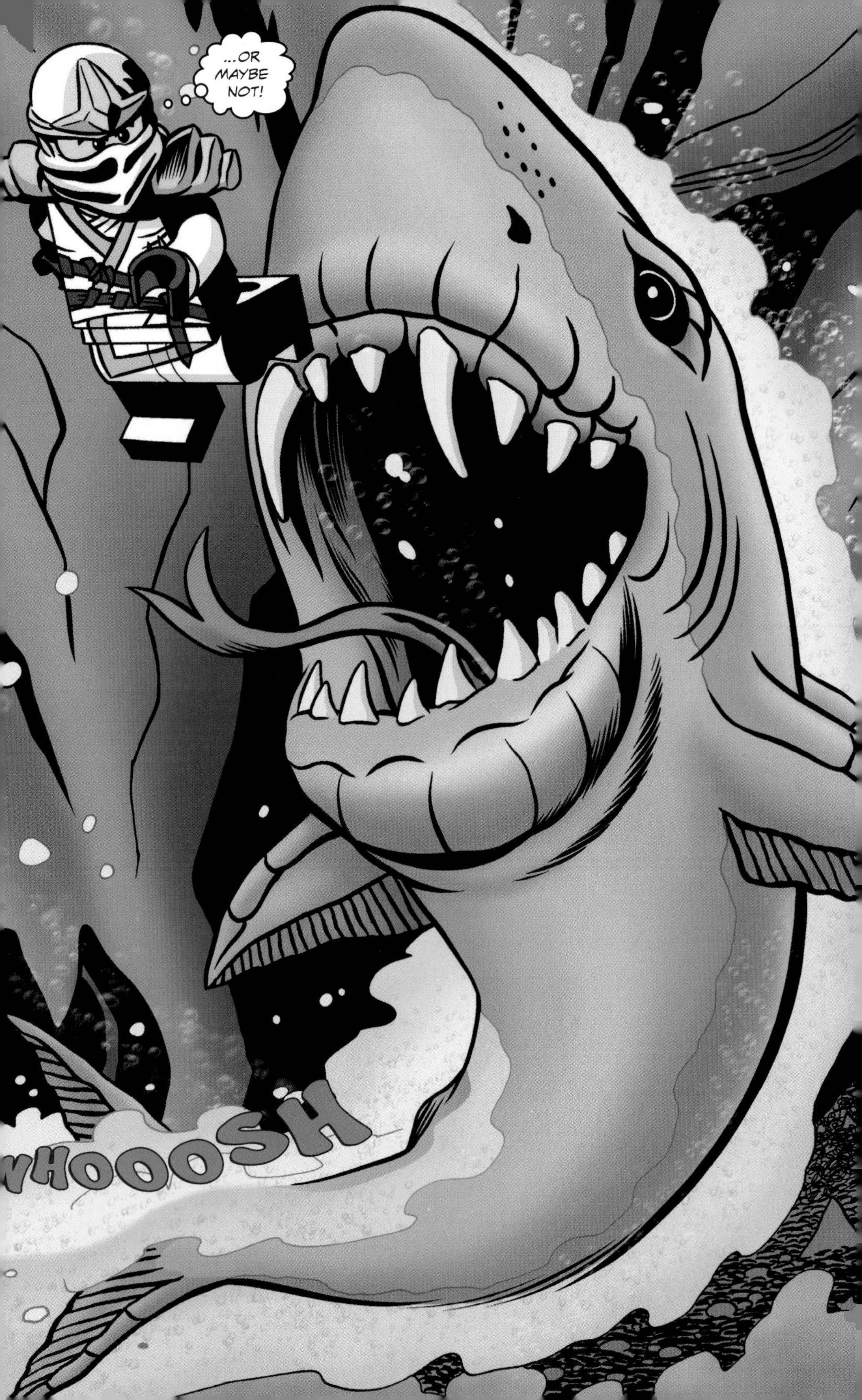
...OR MAYBE NOT!
WHOOOOSH

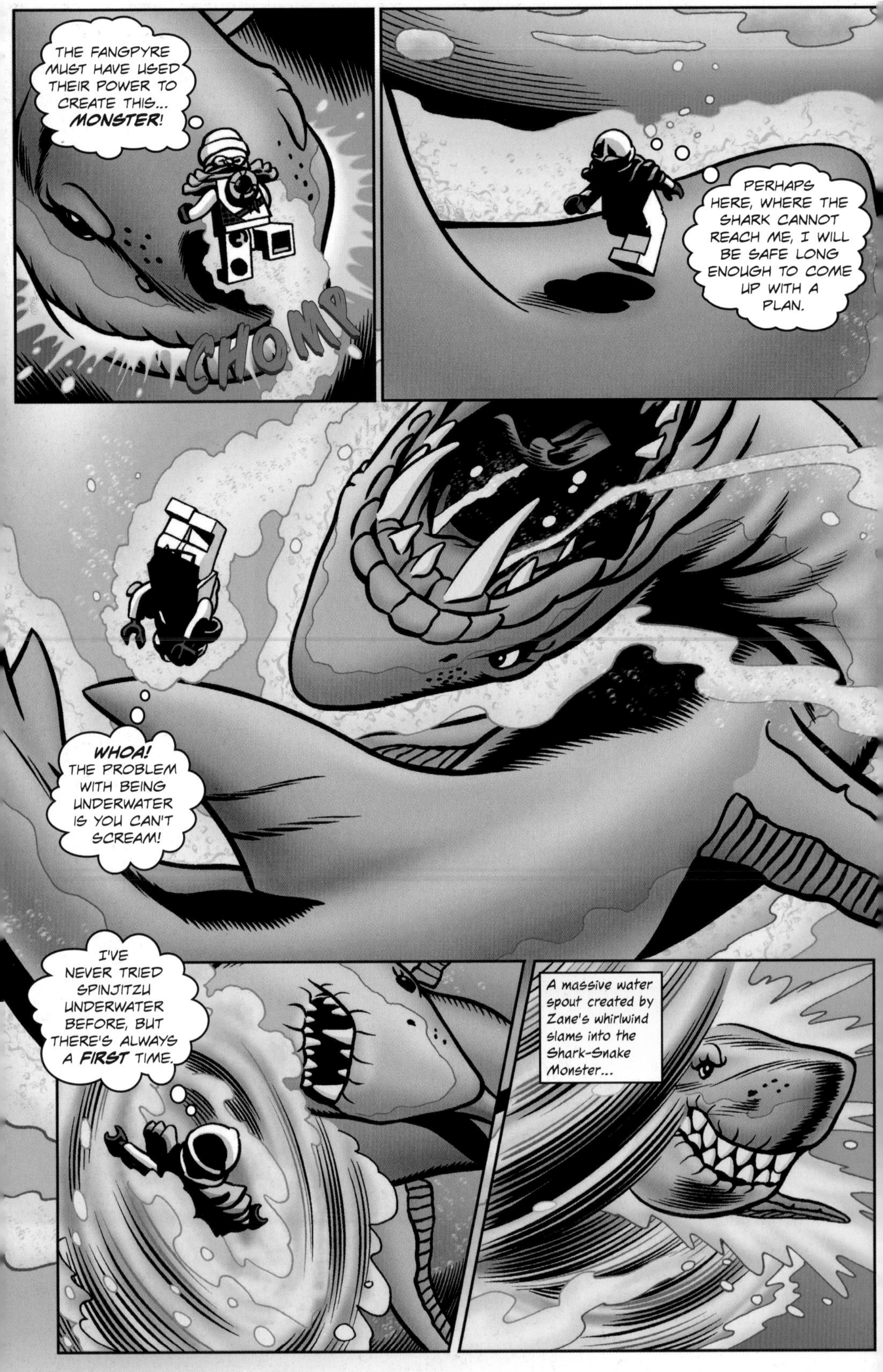
THE FANGPYRE MUST HAVE USED THEIR POWER TO CREATE THIS... MONSTER!
CHOMP
PERHAPS HERE, WHERE THE SHARK CANNOT REACH ME, I WILL BE SAFE LONG ENOUGH TO COME UP WITH A PLAN.
WHOA! THE PROBLEM WITH BEING UNDERWATER IS YOU CAN'T SCREAM!
I'VE NEVER TRIED SPINJITZU UNDERWATER BEFORE, BUT THERE'S ALWAYS A FIRST TIME.
A massive water spout created by Zane's whirlwind slams into the Shark-Snake Monster...

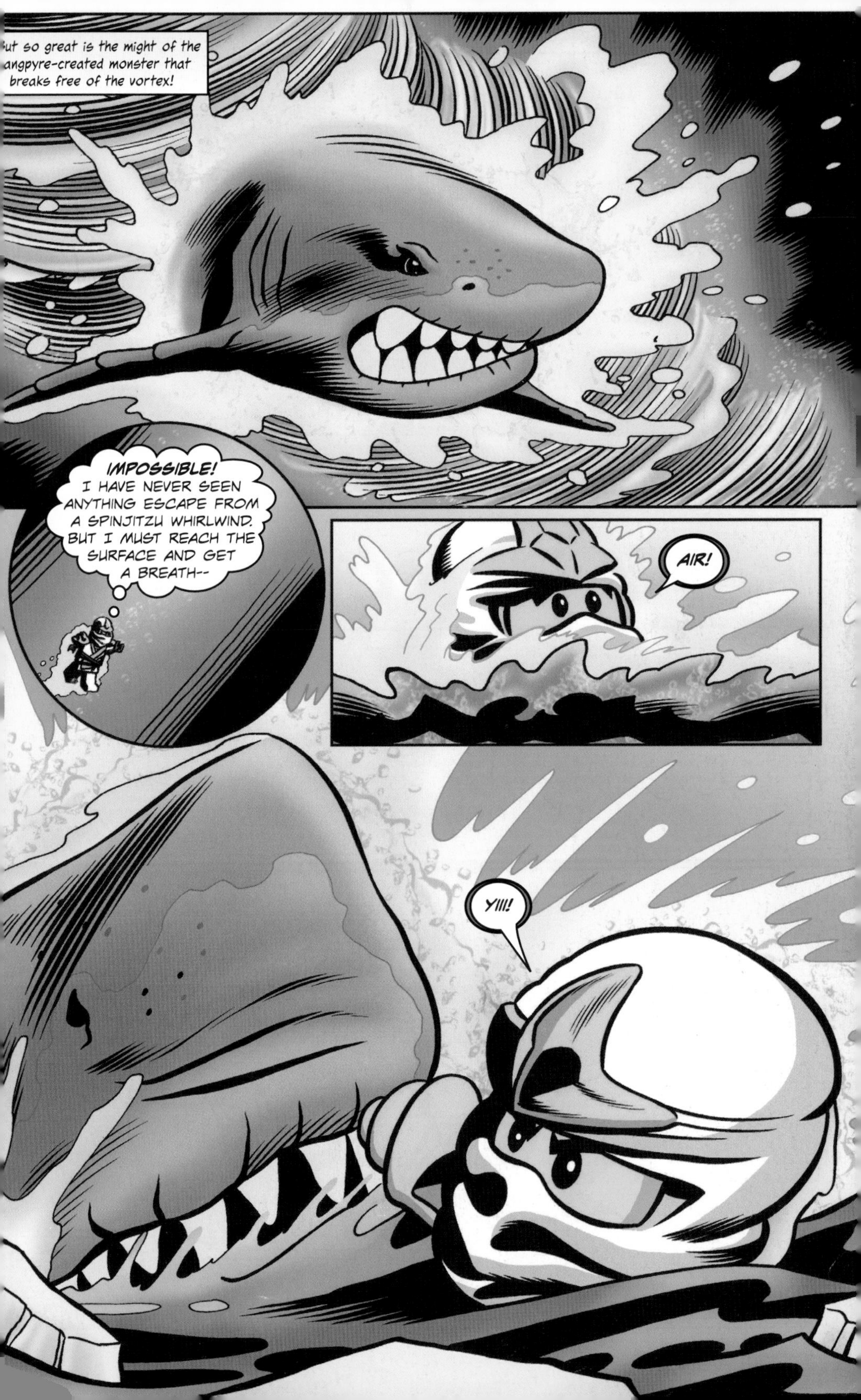
ut so great is the might of the
angpyre-created monster that
breaks free of the vortex!
IMPOSSIBLE! I HAVE NEVER SEEN ANYTHING ESCAPE FROM A SPINJITZU WHIRLWIND. BUT I MUST REACH THE SURFACE AND GET A BREATH--
AIR!
YIII!

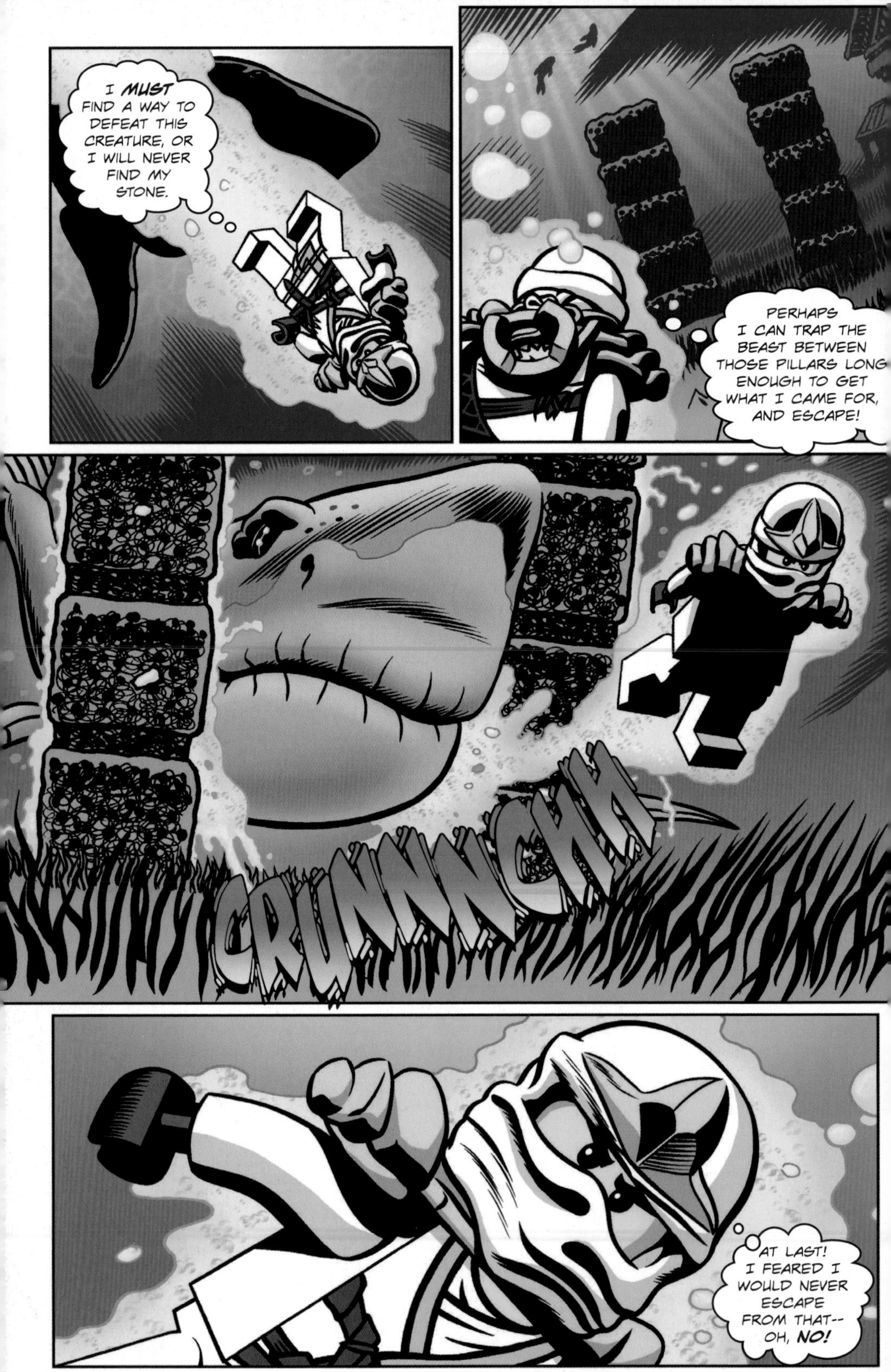
I MUST FIND A WAY TO DEFEAT THIS CREATURE, OR I WILL NEVER FIND MY STONE.
PERHAPS I CAN TRAP THE BEAST BETWEEN THOSE PILLARS LONG ENOUGH TO GET WHAT I CAME FOR, AND ESCAPE!
CRUNNNCHH
AT LAST! I FEARED I WOULD NEVER ESCAPE FROM THAT-- OH, NO!

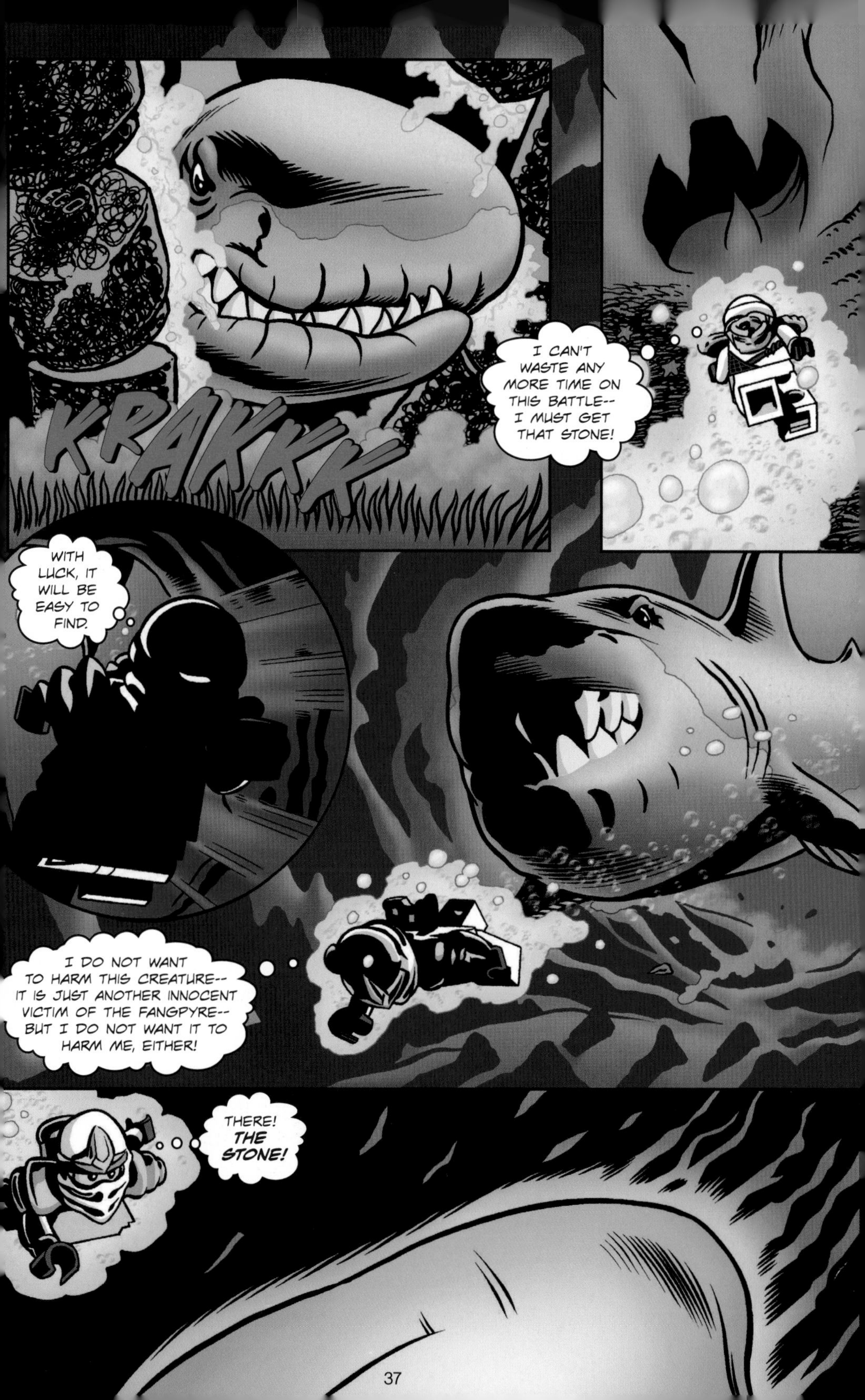
KRAKKK
I CAN'T WASTE ANY MORE TIME ON THIS BATTLE-- I MUST GET THAT STONE!
WITH LUCK, IT WILL BE EASY TO FIND.
I DO NOT WANT TO HARM THIS CREATURE-- IT IS JUST ANOTHER INNOCENT VICTIM OF THE FANGPYRE-- BUT I DO NOT WANT IT TO HARM ME, EITHER!
THERE! THE STONE!

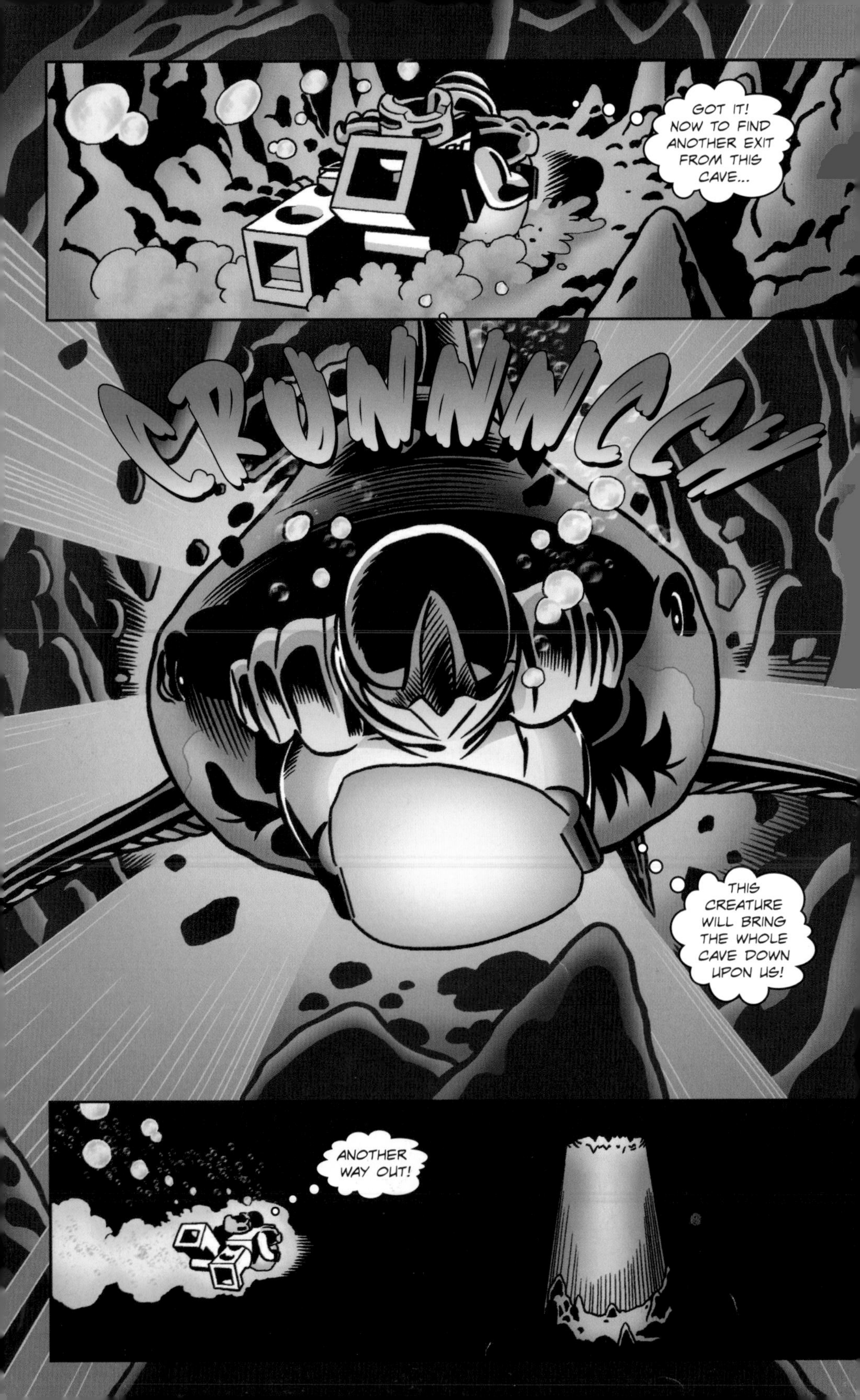
GOT IT! NOW TO FIND ANOTHER EXIT FROM THIS CAVE...
CRUNNNCCH
THIS CREATURE WILL BRING THE WHOLE CAVE DOWN UPON US!
ANOTHER WAY OUT!

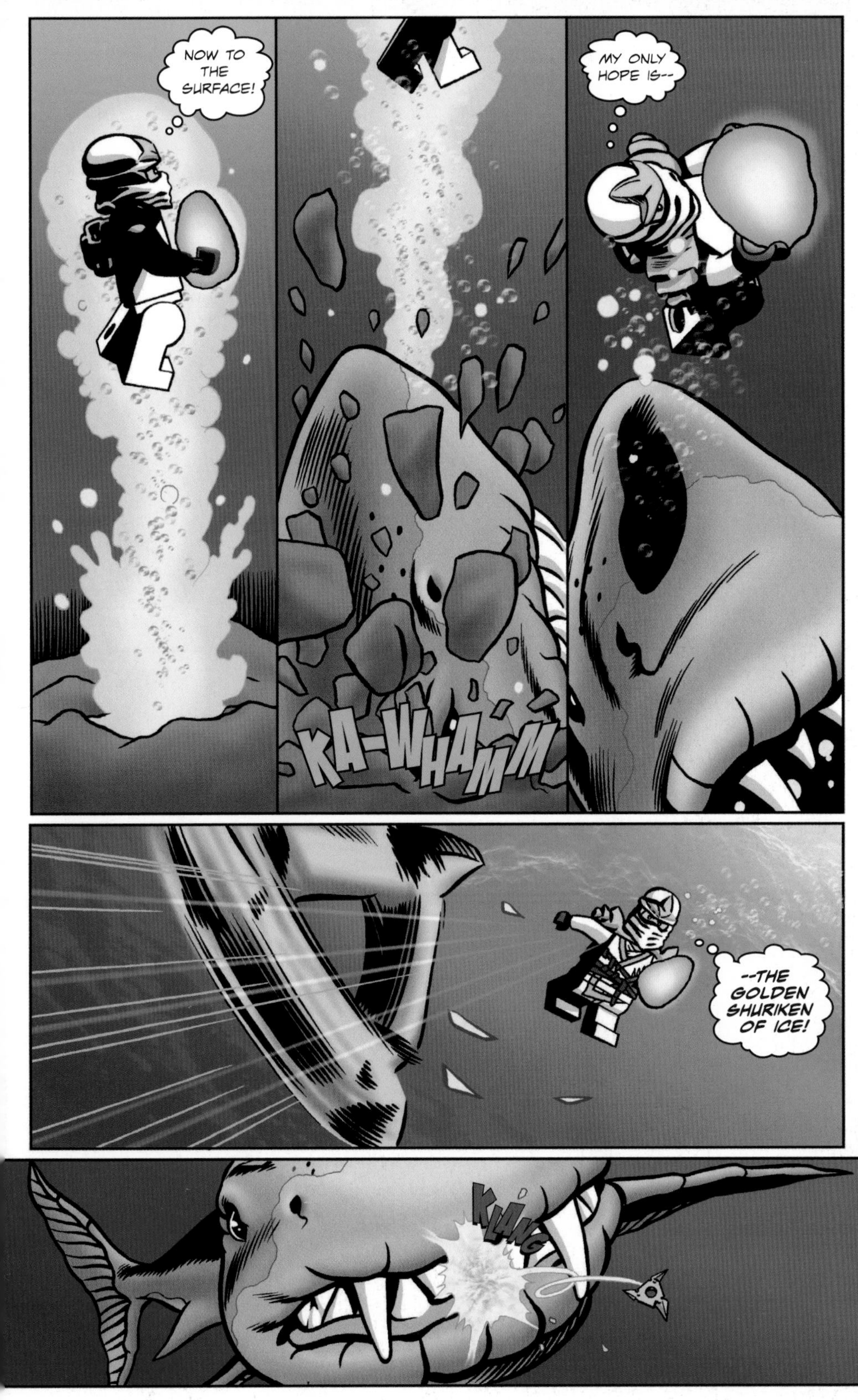
NOW TO THE SURFACE!
KA-WHAMM
MY ONLY HOPE IS--
--THE GOLDEN SHURIKEN OF ICE!
KLANG

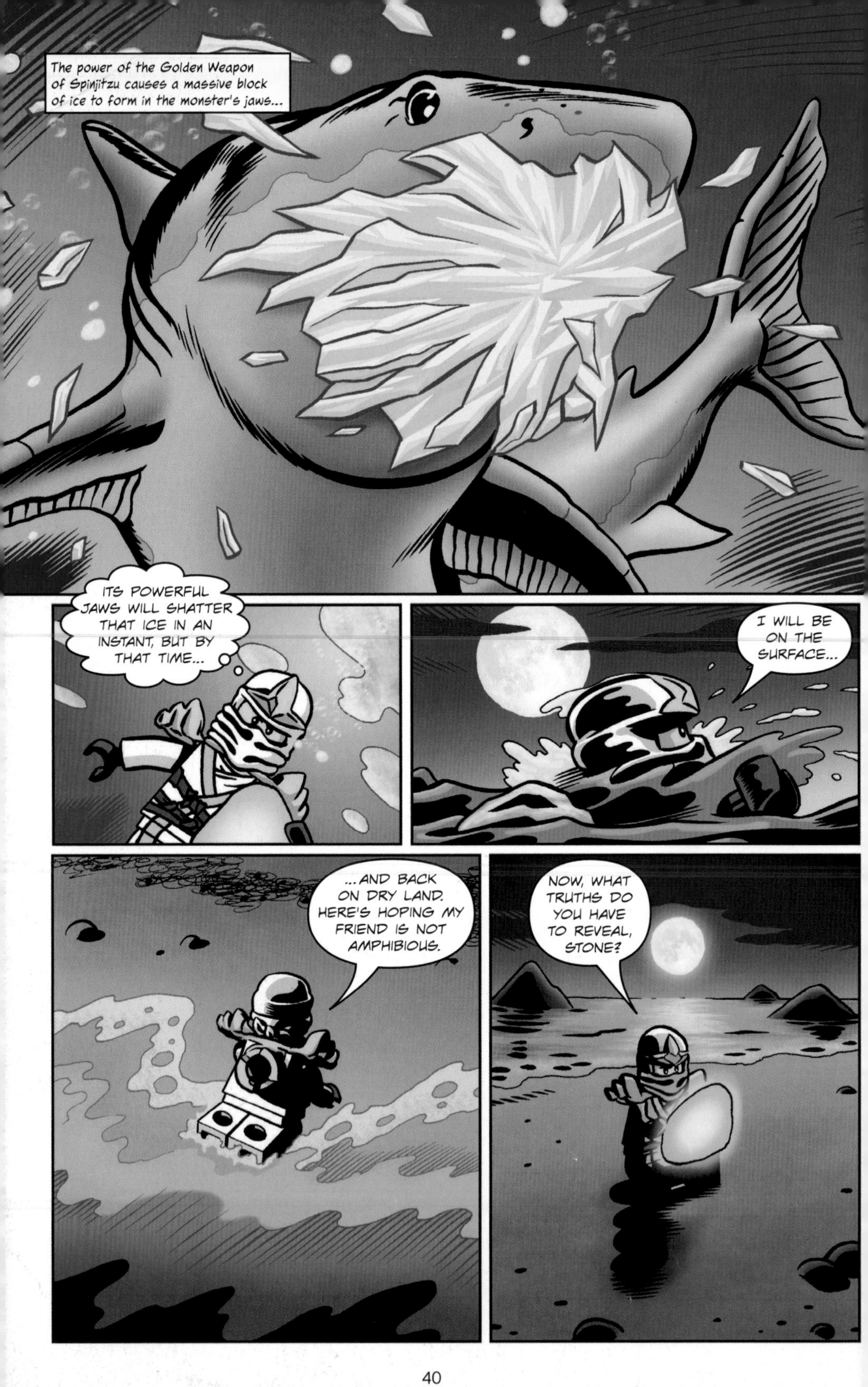
The power of the Golden Weapon of Spinjitzu causes a massive block of ice to form in the monster's jaws...
ITS POWERFUL JAWS WILL SHATTER THAT ICE IN AN INSTANT, BUT BY THAT TIME...
I WILL BE ON THE SURFACE...
...AND BACK ON DRY LAND. HERE'S HOPING MY FRIEND IS NOT AMPHIBIOUS.
NOW, WHAT TRUTHS DO YOU HAVE TO REVEAL, STONE?

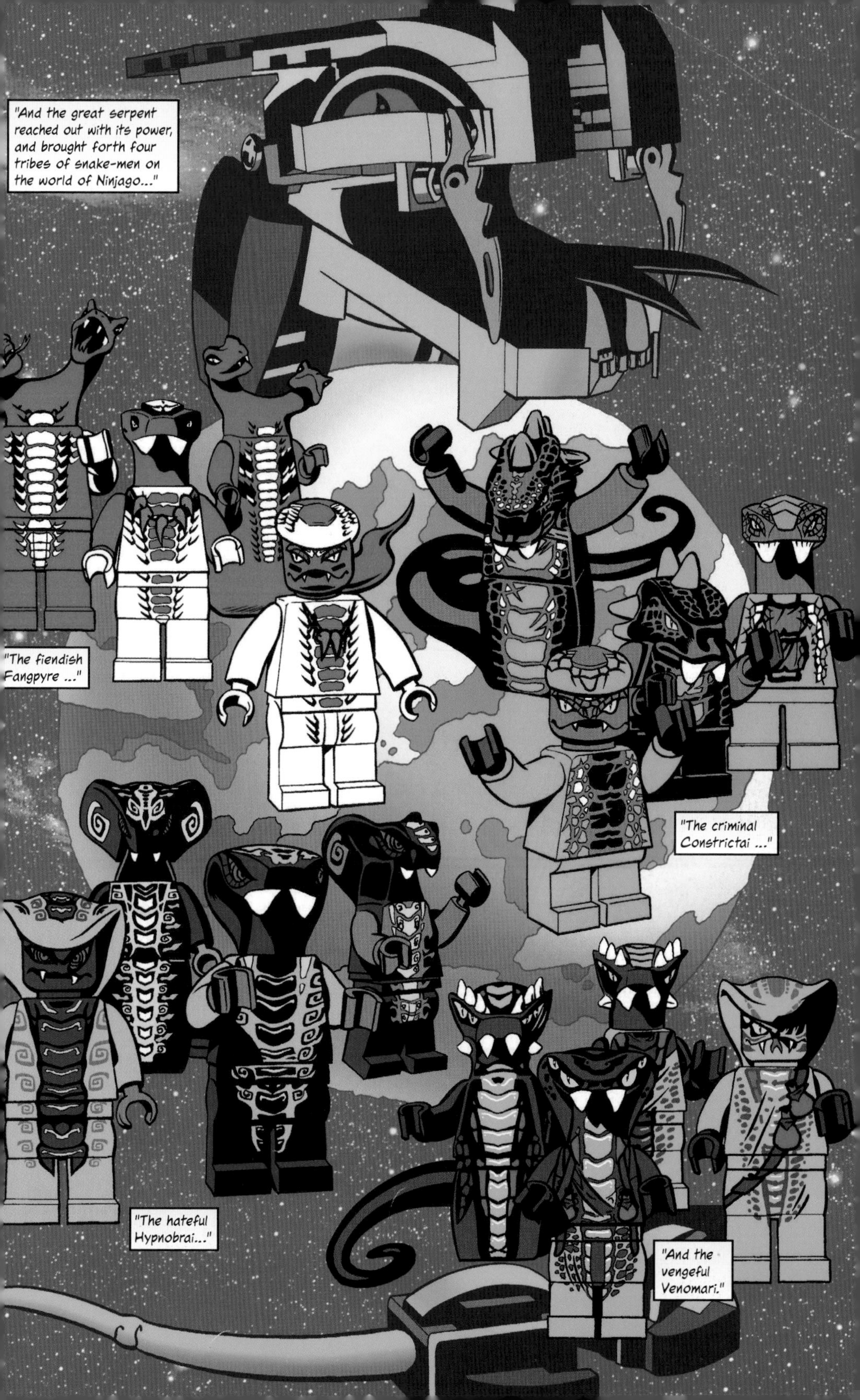
"And the great serpent reached out with its power, and brought forth four tribes of snake-men on the world of Ninjago..."
"The fiendish Fangpyre ..."
"The criminal Constrictai ..."
"The hateful Hypnobrai..."
"And the vengeful Venomari."

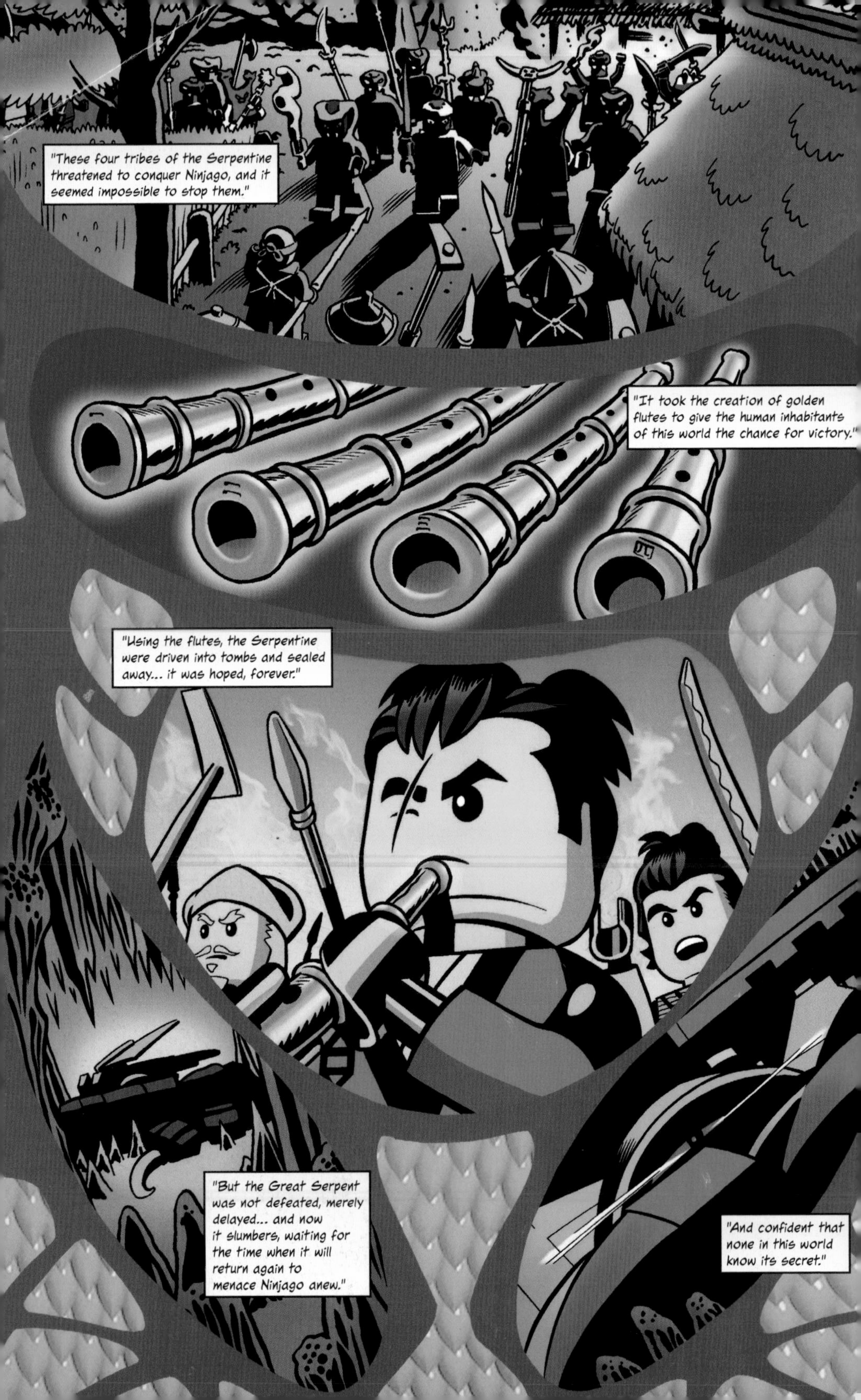
"These four tribes of the Serpentine threatened to conquer Ninjago, and it seemed impossible to stop them."
"It took the creation of golden flutes to give the human inhabitants of this world the chance for victory."
"Using the flutes, the Serpentine were driven into tombs and sealed away... it was hoped, forever."
"But the Great Serpent was not defeated, merely delayed... and now it slumbers, waiting for the time when it will return again to menace Ninjago anew."
"And confident that none in this world know its secret."

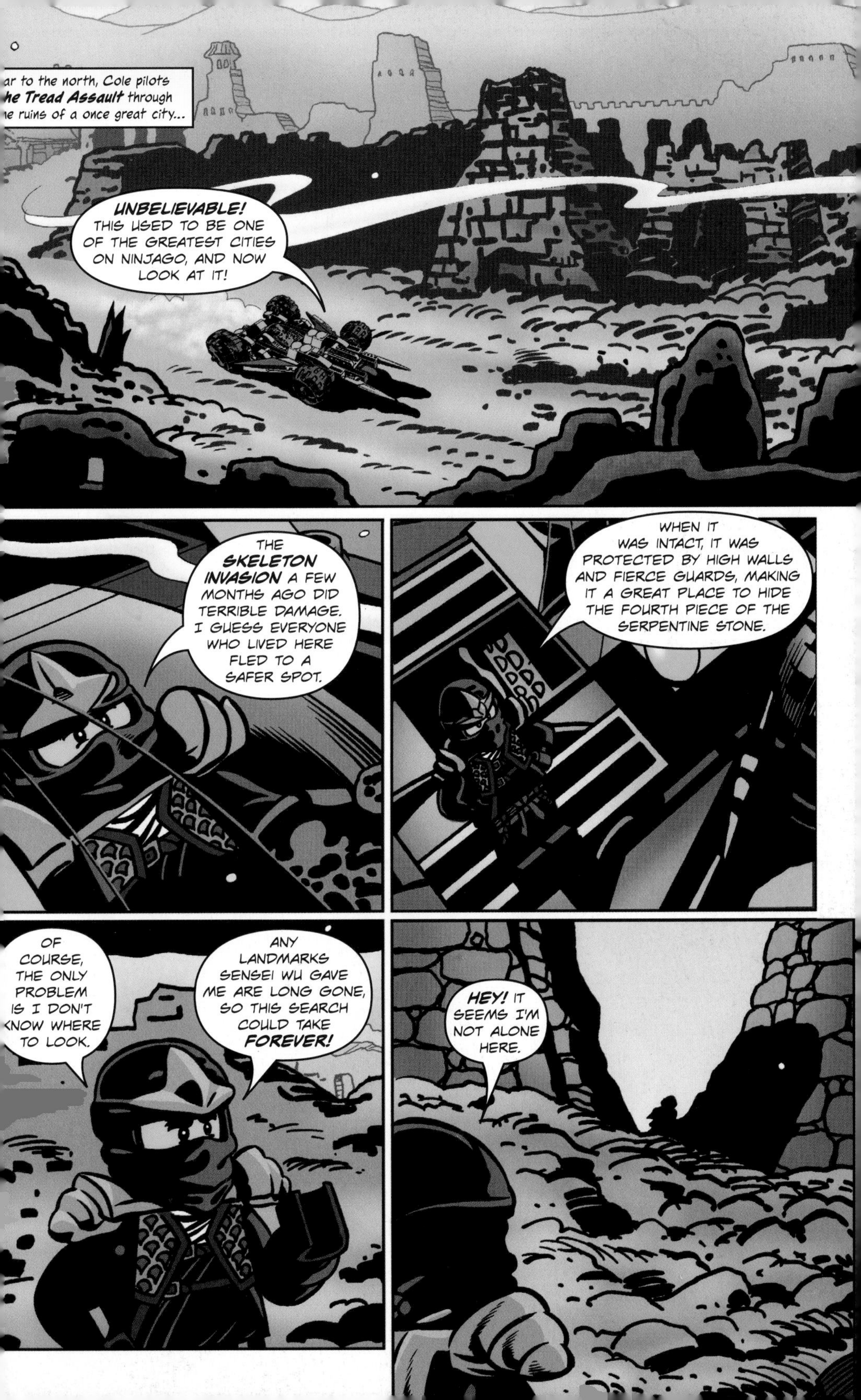
ar to the north, Cole pilots he Tread Assault through e ruins of a once great city...
UNBELIEVABLE! THIS USED TO BE ONE OF THE GREATEST CITIES ON NINJAGO, AND NOW LOOK AT IT!
THE SKELETON INVASION A FEW MONTHS AGO DID TERRIBLE DAMAGE. I GUESS EVERYONE WHO LIVED HERE FLED TO A SAFER SPOT.
WHEN IT WAS INTACT, IT WAS PROTECTED BY HIGH WALLS AND FIERCE GUARDS, MAKING IT A GREAT PLACE TO HIDE THE FOURTH PIECE OF THE SERPENTINE STONE.
OF COURSE, THE ONLY PROBLEM IS I DON'T KNOW WHERE TO LOOK.
ANY LANDMARKS SENSEI WU GAVE ME ARE LONG GONE, SO THIS SEARCH COULD TAKE FOREVER!
HEY! IT SEEMS I'M NOT ALONE HERE.

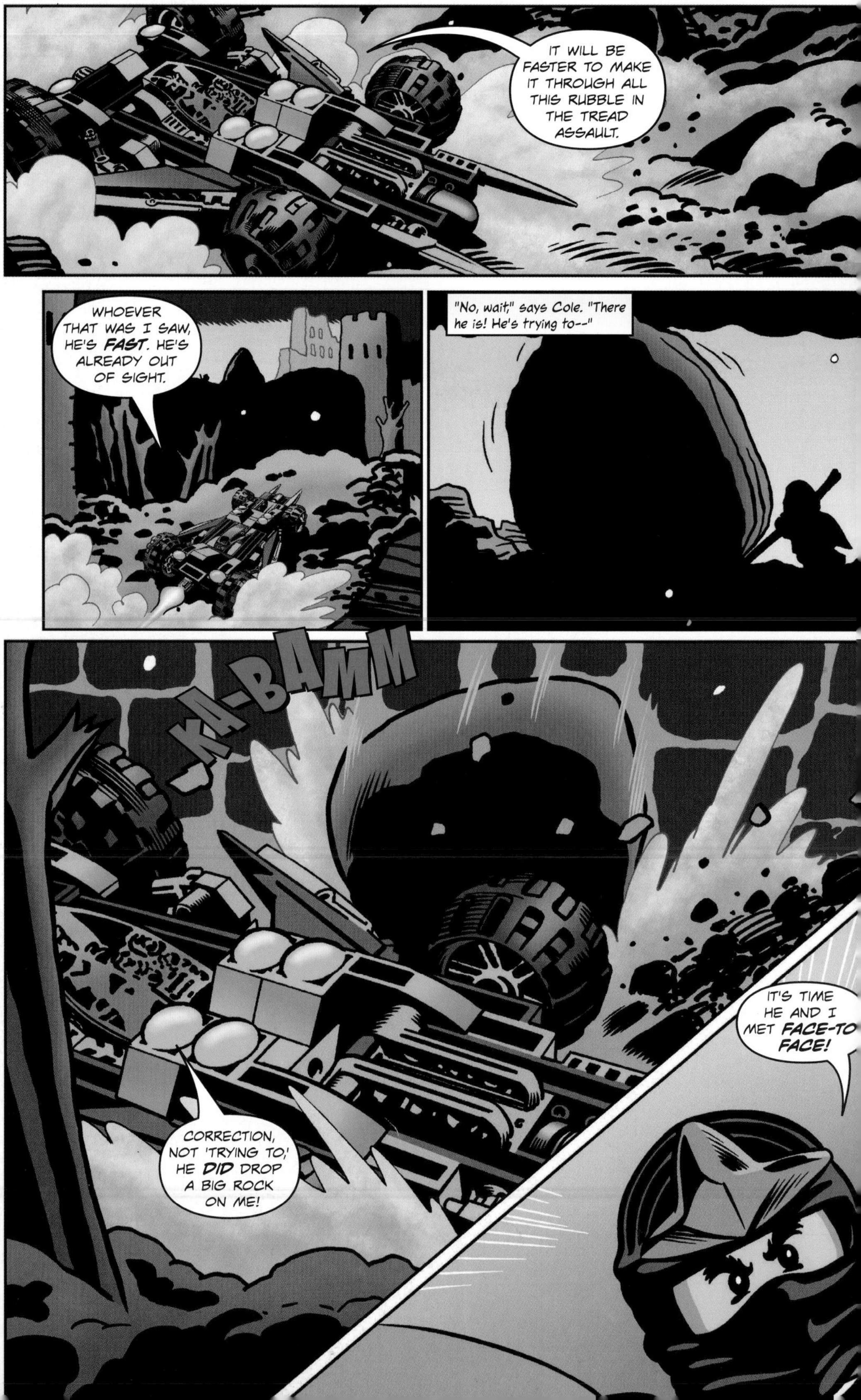
IT WILL BE FASTER TO MAKE IT THROUGH ALL THIS RUBBLE IN THE TREAD ASSAULT.
WHOEVER THAT WAS I SAW, HE'S FAST. HE'S ALREADY OUT OF SIGHT.
"No, wait," says Cole. "There he is! He's trying to--"
KA-BAMM
CORRECTION, NOT 'TRYING TO,' HE DID DROP A BIG ROCK ON ME!
IT'S TIME HE AND I MET FACE-TO FACE!

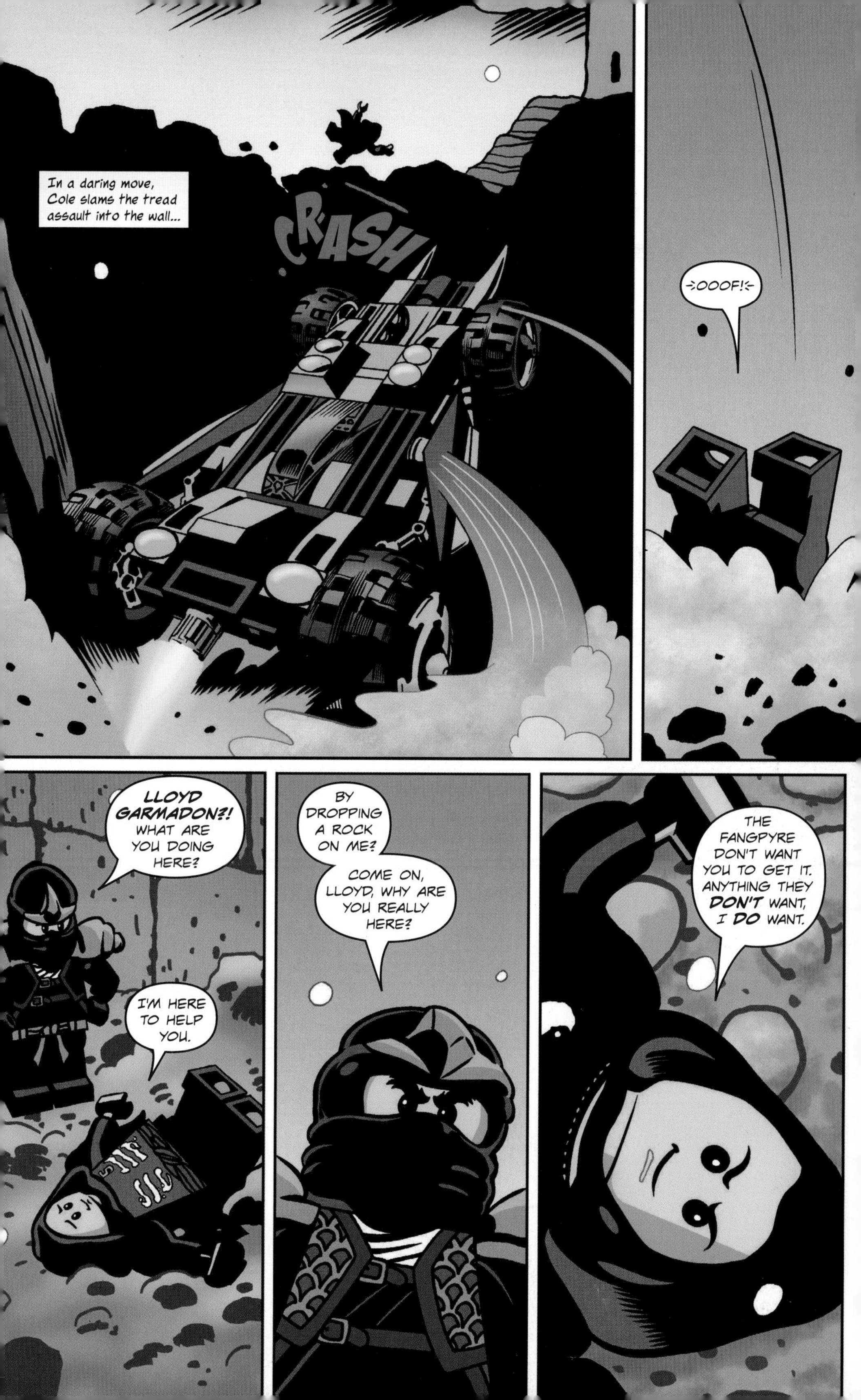
In a daring move, Cole slams the tread assault into the wall...
CRASH
OOOF!
LLOYD GARMADON?! WHAT ARE YOU DOING HERE?
I'M HERE TO HELP YOU.
BY DROPPING A ROCK ON ME?
COME ON, LLOYD, WHY ARE YOU REALLY HERE?
THE FANGPYRE DON'T WANT YOU TO GET IT. ANYTHING THEY DON'T WANT, I DO WANT.

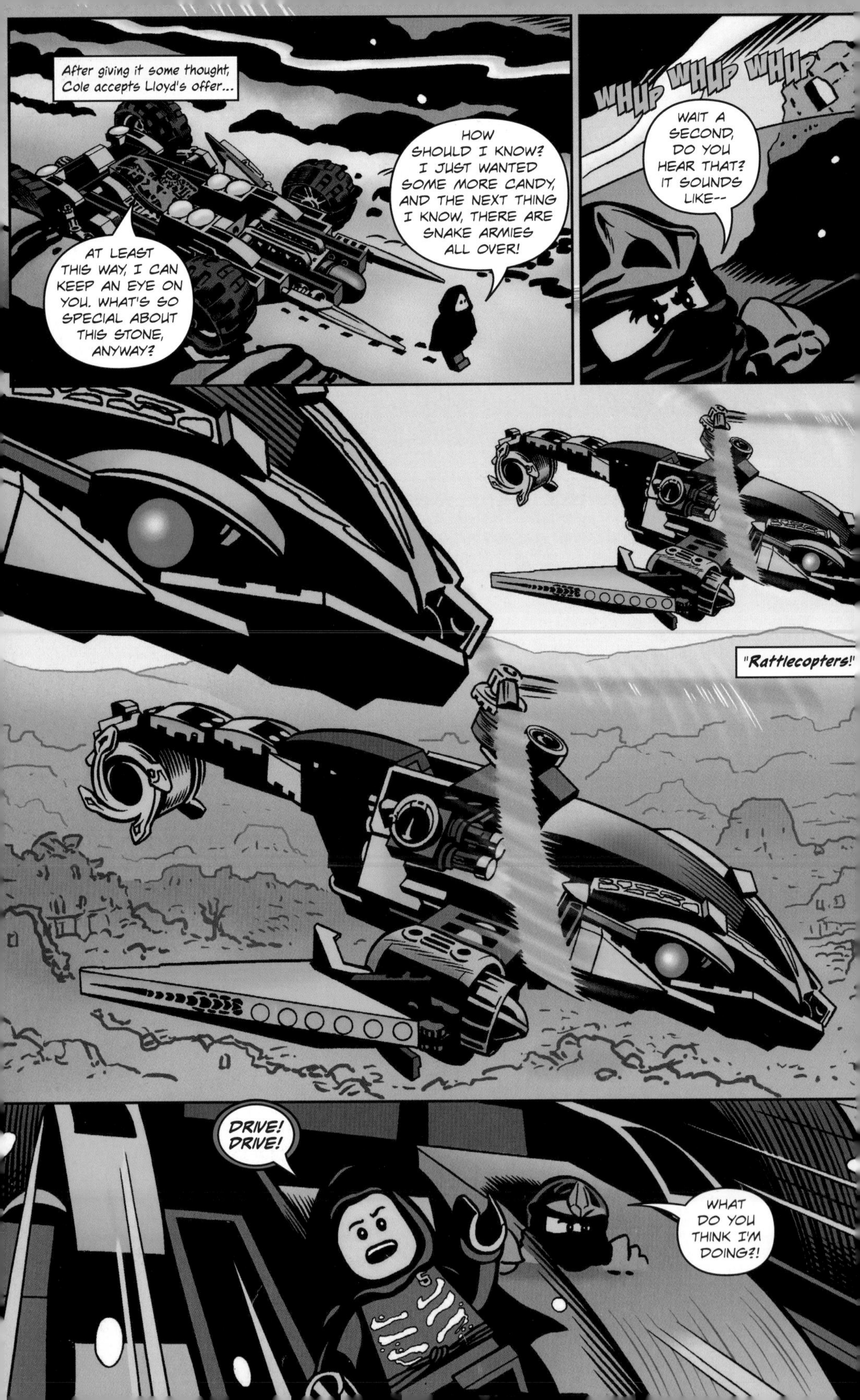
After giving it some thought, Cole accepts Lloyd's offer...
AT LEAST THIS WAY, I CAN KEEP AN EYE ON YOU. WHAT'S SO SPECIAL ABOUT THIS STONE, ANYWAY?
HOW SHOULD I KNOW? I JUST WANTED SOME MORE CANDY, AND THE NEXT THING I KNOW, THERE ARE SNAKE ARMIES ALL OVER!
WHUP WHUP WHUP
WAIT A SECOND, DO YOU HEAR THAT? IT SOUNDS LIKE--
"Rattlecopters!"
DRIVE! DRIVE!
WHAT DO YOU THINK I'M DOING?!

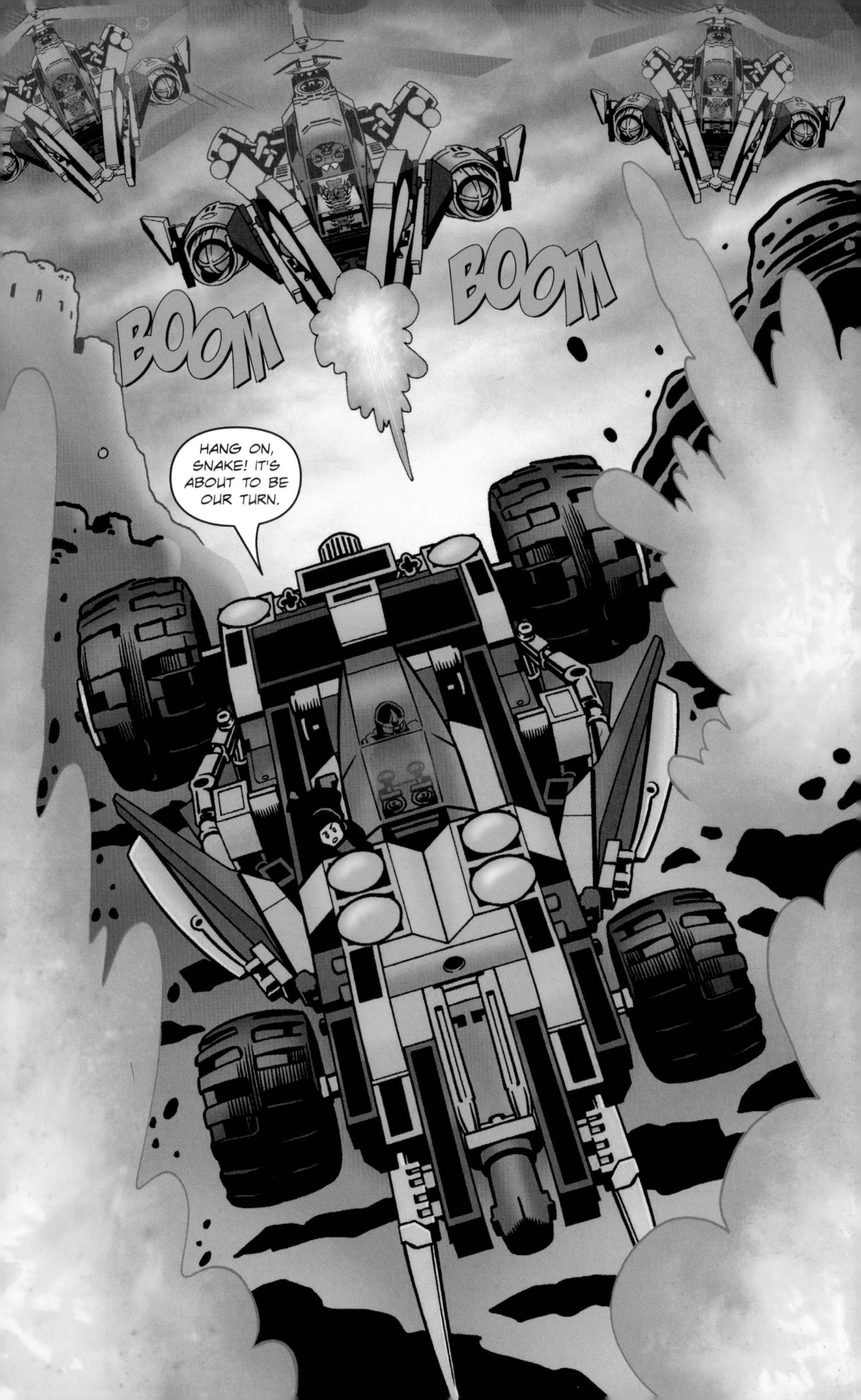
BOOM
BOOM
HANG ON, SNAKE! IT'S ABOUT TO BE OUR TURN.

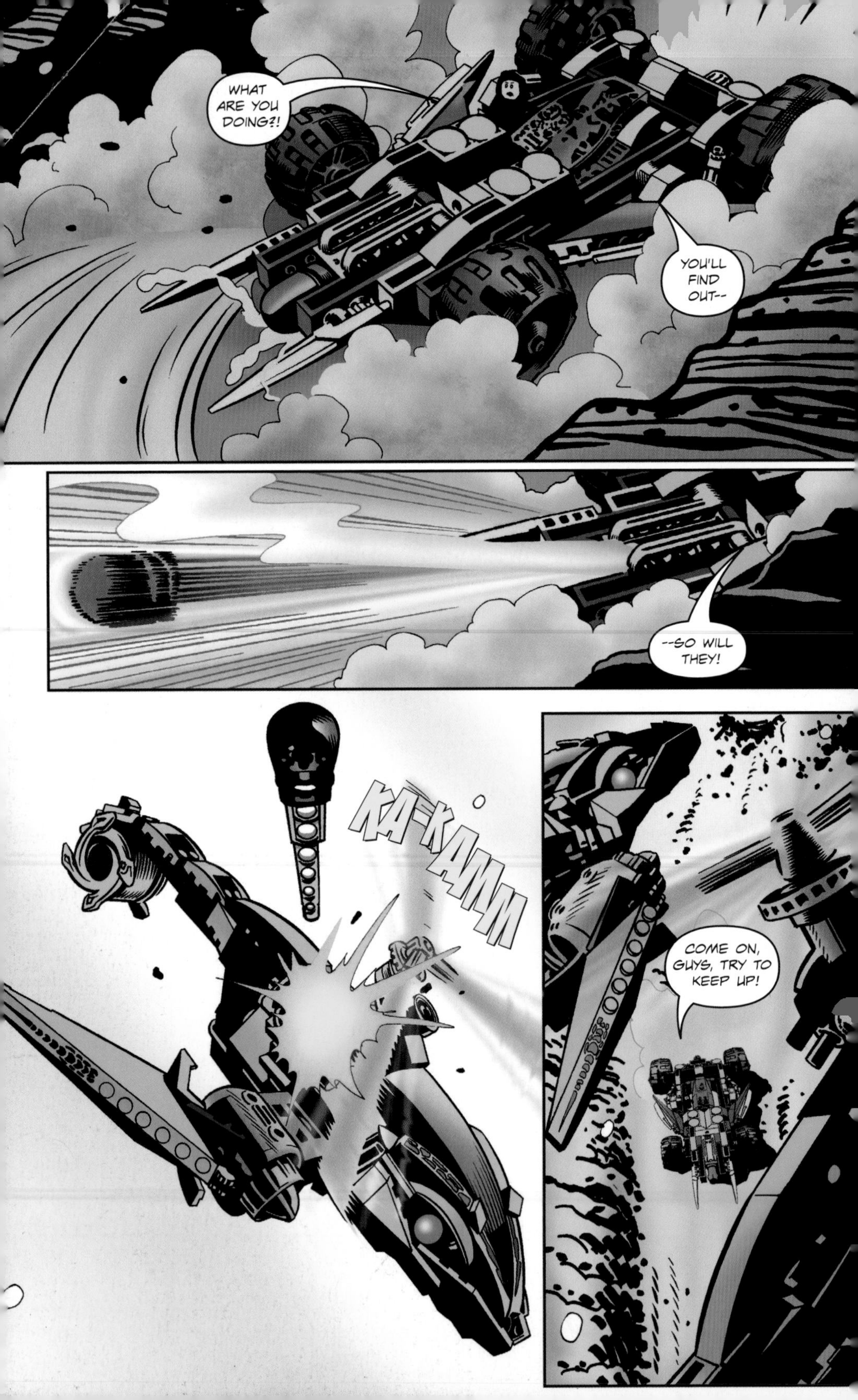
WHAT ARE YOU DOING?!
YOU'LL FIND OUT--
--SO WILL THEY!
KA-KAMM
COME ON, GUYS, TRY TO KEEP UP!

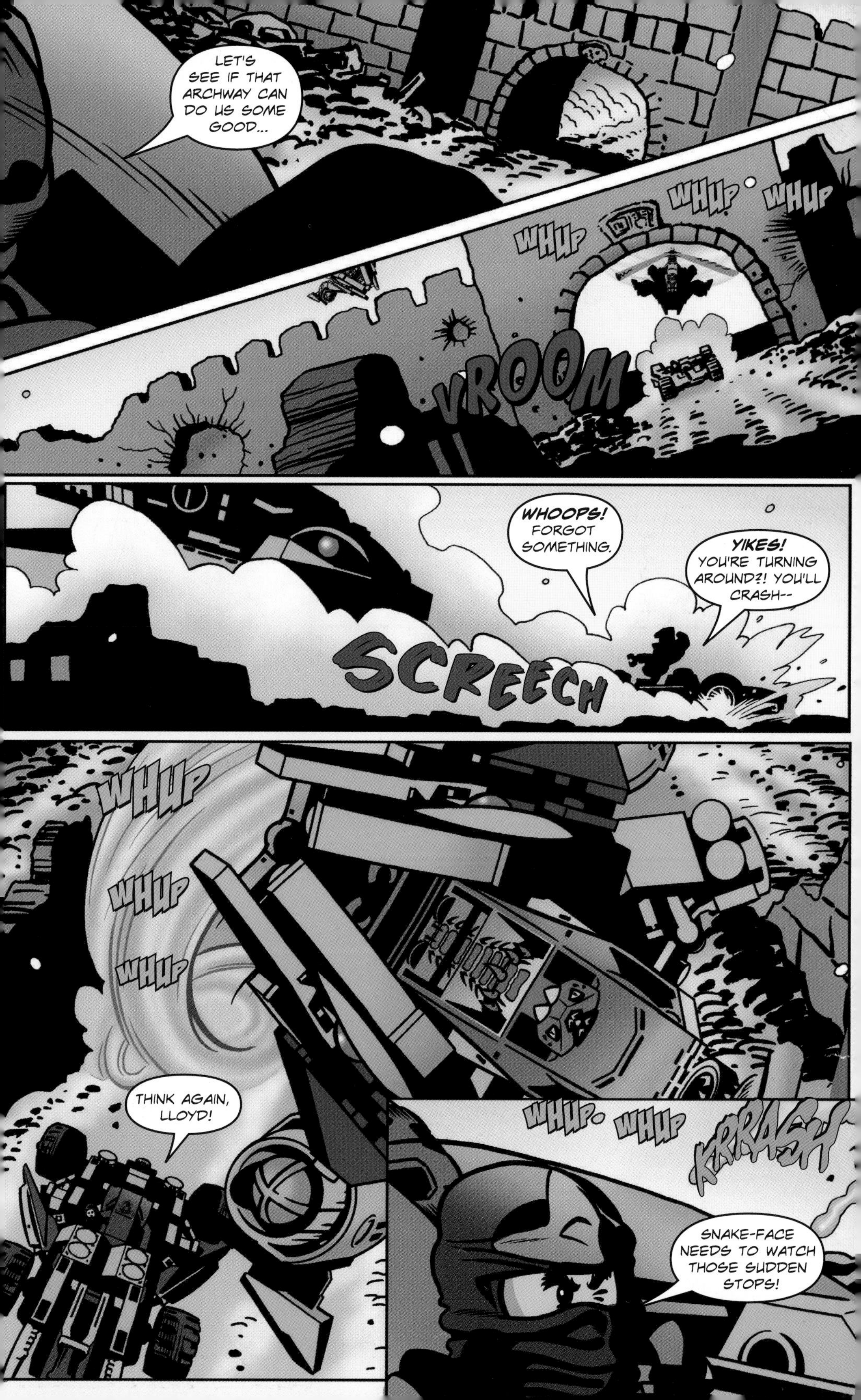
LET'S SEE IF THAT ARCHWAY CAN DO US SOME GOOD...
WHUP
WHUP
WHUP
VROOM
WHOOPS! FORGOT SOMETHING.
YIKES! YOU'RE TURNING AROUND?! YOU'LL CRASH--
SCREECH
WHUP
WHUP
WHUP
THINK AGAIN, LLOYD!
WHUP
WHUP
KRASH
SNAKE-FACE NEEDS TO WATCH THOSE SUDDEN STOPS!

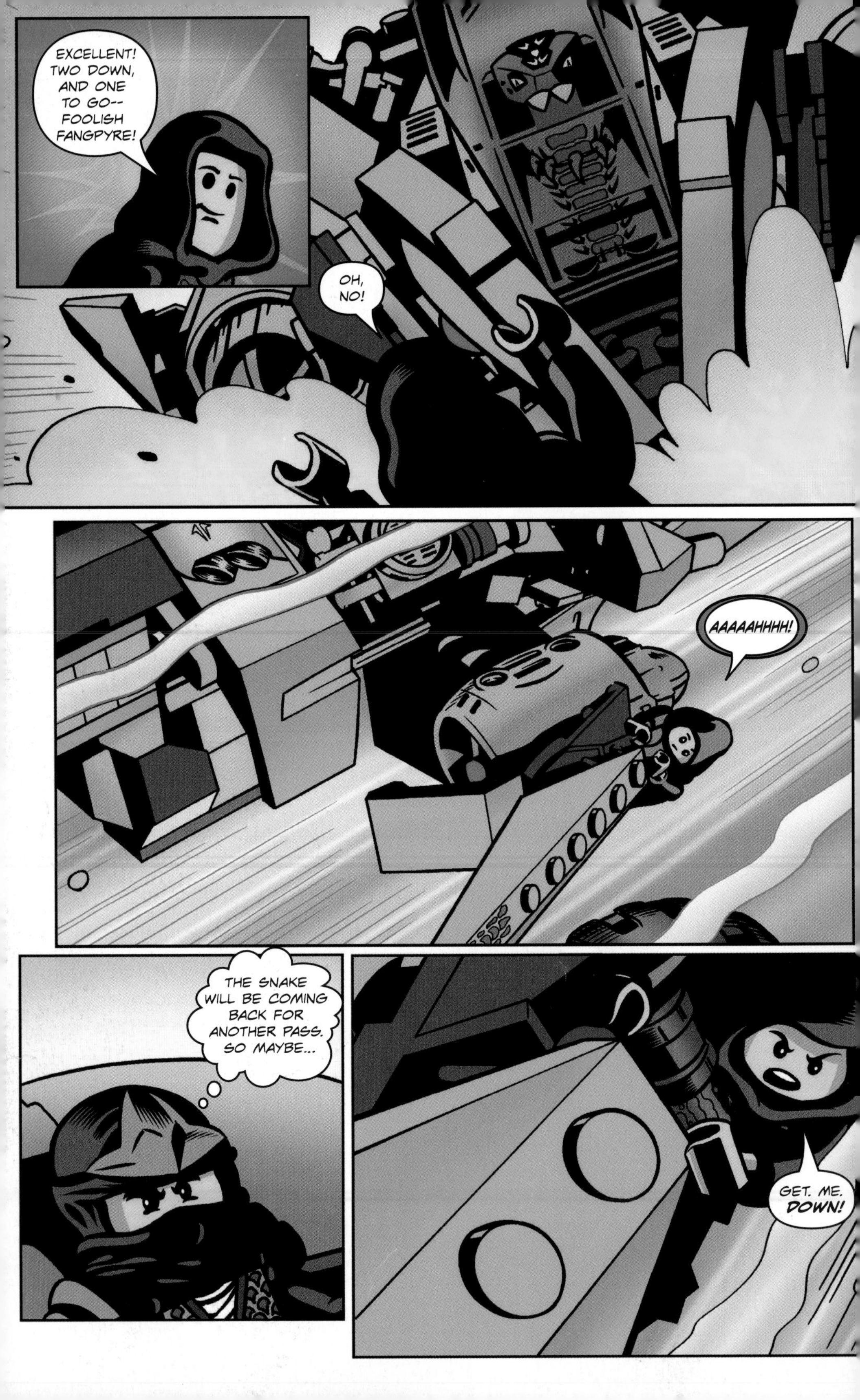
EXCELLENT! TWO DOWN, AND ONE TO GO-- FOOLISH FANGPYRE!
OH, NO!
AAAAAHHHH!
THE SNAKE WILL BE COMING BACK FOR ANOTHER PASS. SO MAYBE...
GET. ME. DOWN!

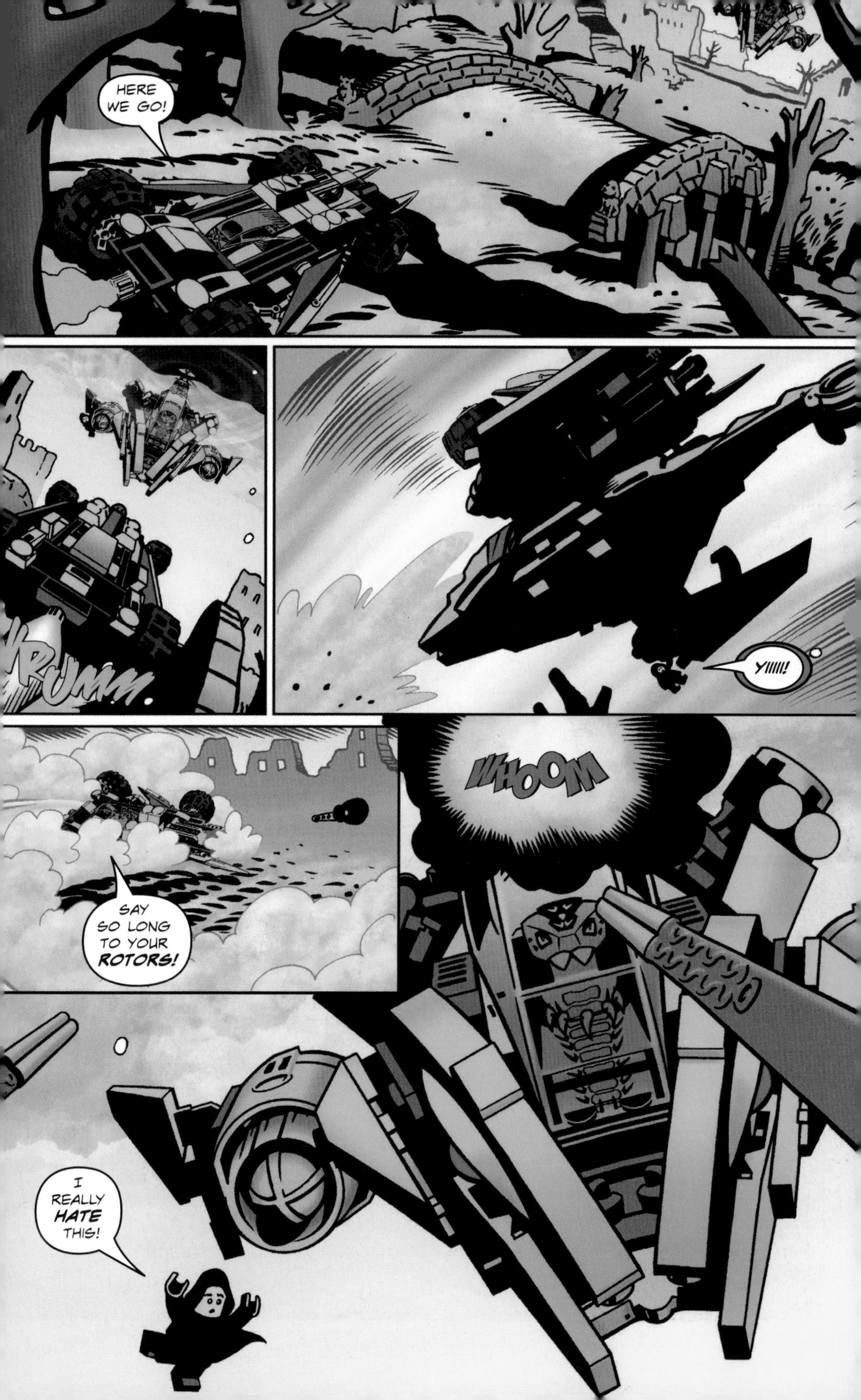
HERE WE GO!
KRUMM
YIIII!
SAY SO LONG TO YOUR ROTORS!
WHOOM
I REALLY HATE THIS!

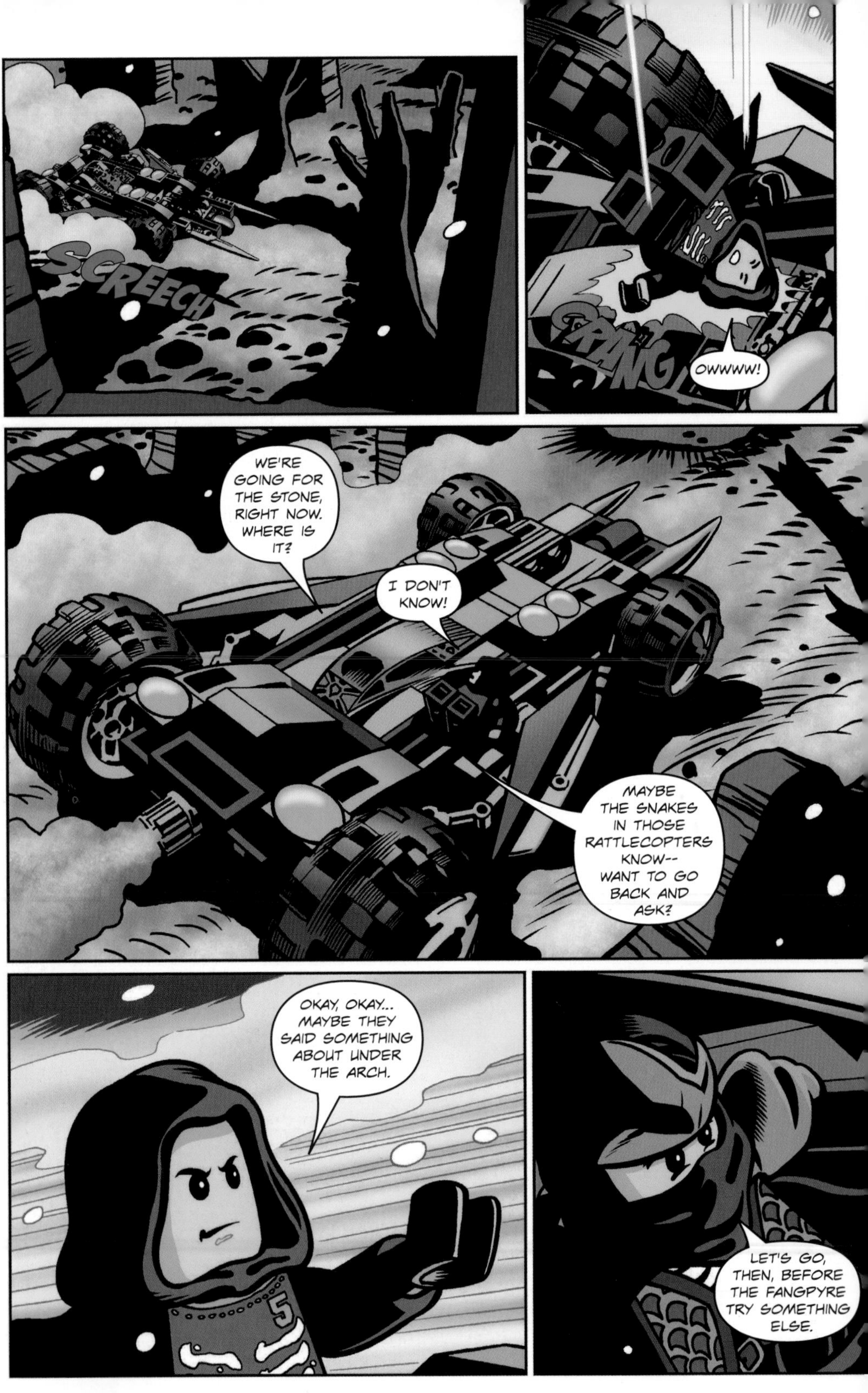
SCREECH
CRANG
OWWWW!
WE'RE GOING FOR THE STONE, RIGHT NOW. WHERE IS IT?
I DON'T KNOW!
MAYBE THE SNAKES IN THOSE RATTLECOPTERS KNOW-- WANT TO GO BACK AND ASK?
OKAY, OKAY... MAYBE THEY SAID SOMETHING ABOUT UNDER THE ARCH.
LET'S GO, THEN, BEFORE THE FANGPYRE TRY SOMETHING ELSE.

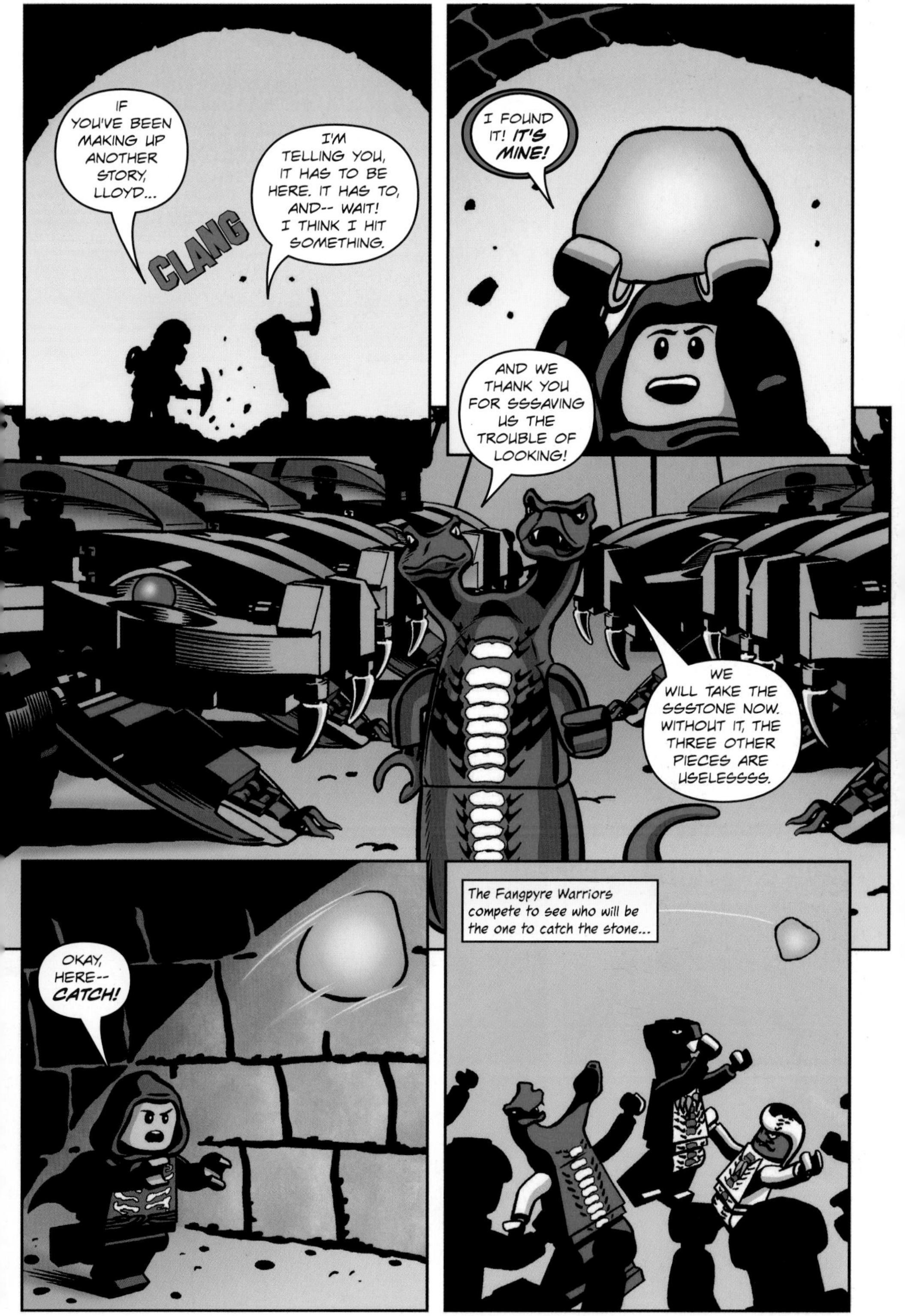

IF YOU'VE BEEN MAKING UP ANOTHER STORY, LLOYD...
CLANG
I'M TELLING YOU, IT HAS TO BE HERE. IT HAS TO, AND-- WAIT! I THINK I HIT SOMETHING.
I FOUND IT! IT'S MINE!
AND WE THANK YOU FOR SSSAVING US THE TROUBLE OF LOOKING!
WE WILL TAKE THE SSSTONE NOW. WITHOUT IT, THE THREE OTHER PIECES ARE USELESSSS.
OKAY, HERE-- CATCH!
The Fangpyre Warriors compete to see who will be the one to catch the stone...

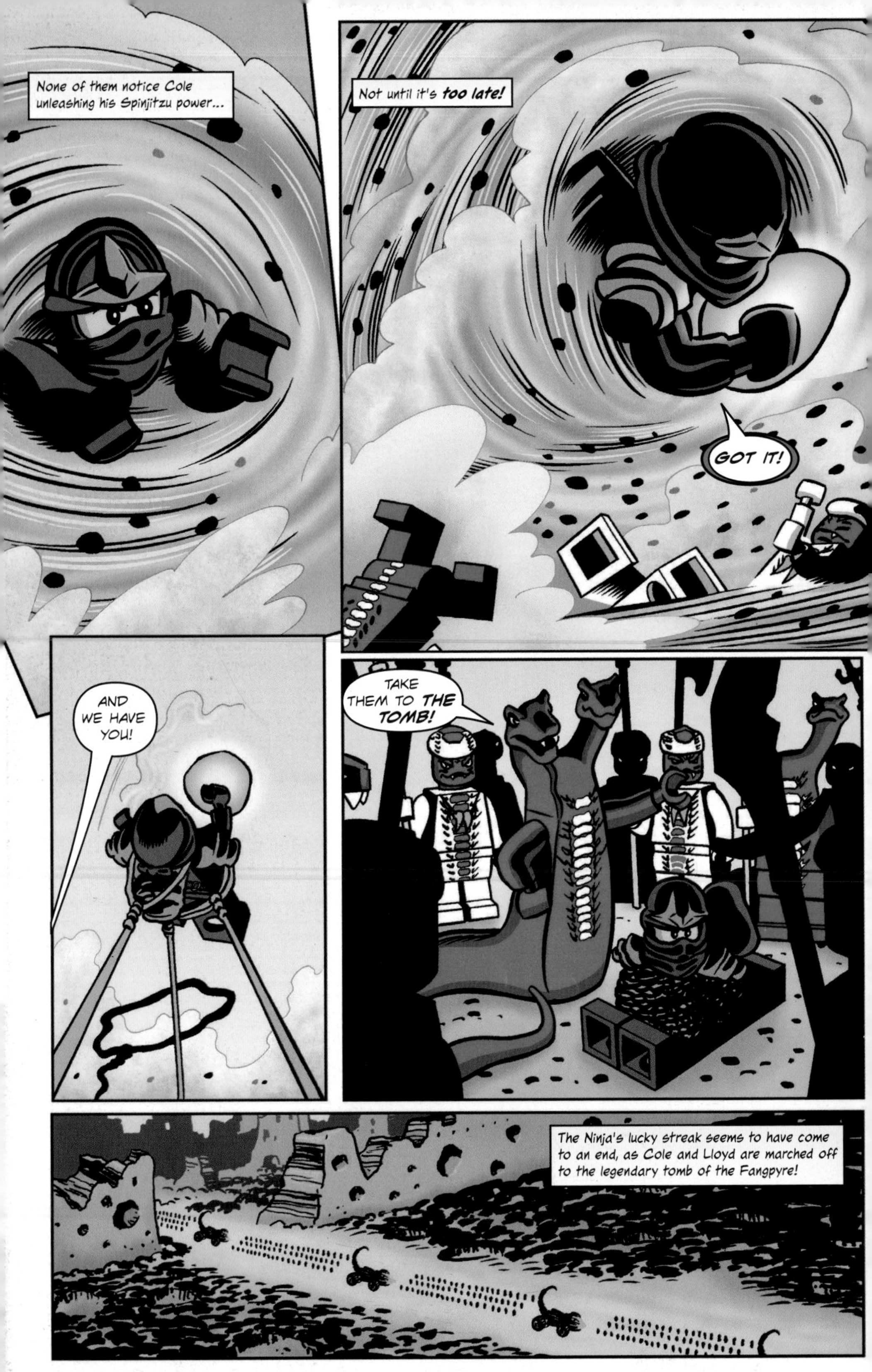
None of them notice Cole unleashing his Spinjitzu power...
Not until it's too late!
GOT IT!
AND WE HAVE YOU!
TAKE THEM TO THE TOMB!
The Ninja's lucky streak seems to have come to an end, as Cole and Lloyd are marched off to the legendary tomb of the Fangpyre!

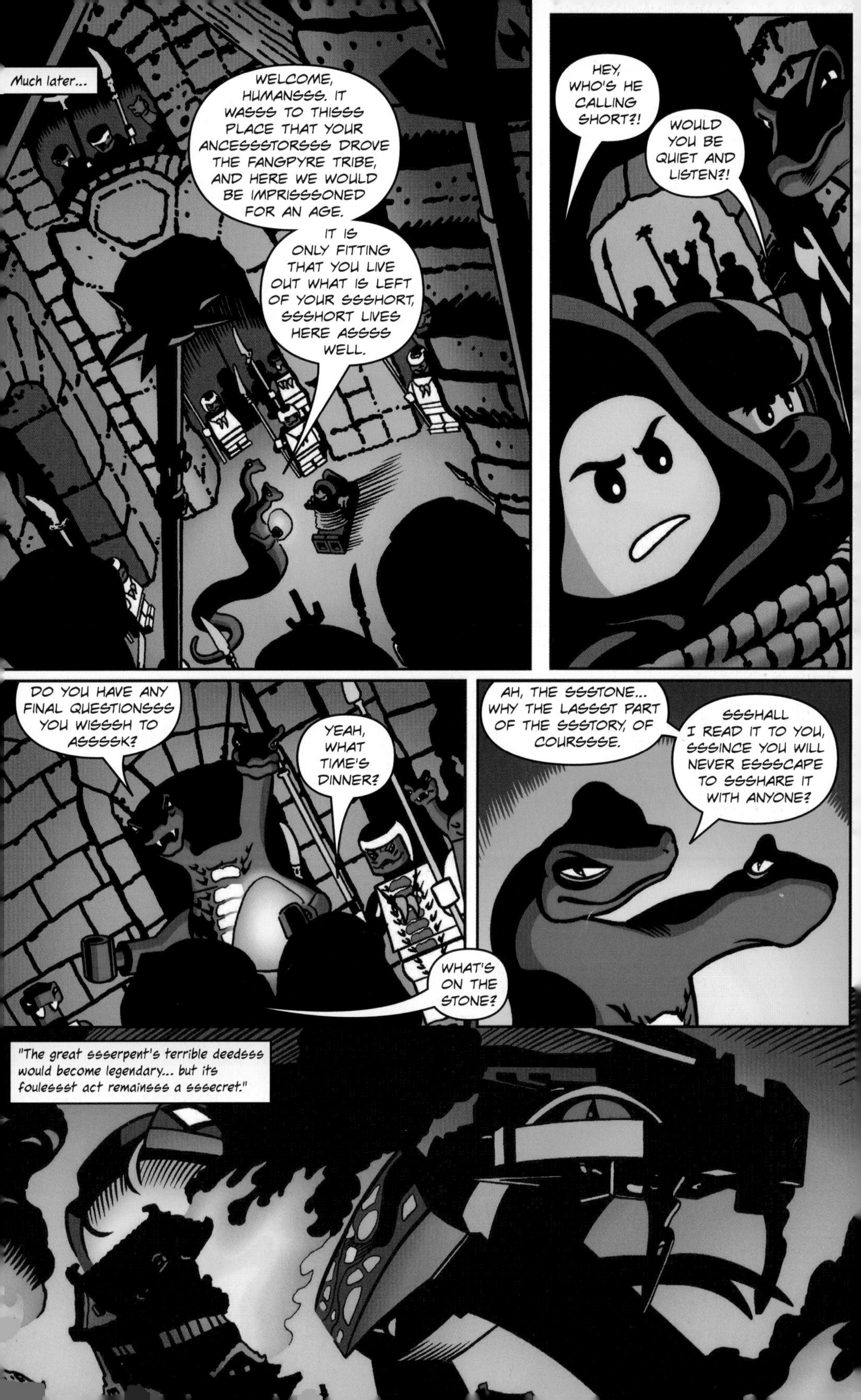
Much later...
WELCOME, HUMANSSS. IT WASSS TO THISSS PLACE THAT YOUR ANCESSSTORSSS DROVE THE FANGPYRE TRIBE, AND HERE WE WOULD BE IMPRISSSONED FOR AN AGE.
IT IS ONLY FITTING THAT YOU LIVE OUT WHAT IS LEFT OF YOUR SSSHORT, SSSHORT LIVES HERE ASSSS WELL.
HEY, WHO'S HE CALLING SHORT?!
WOULD YOU BE QUIET AND LISTEN?!
DO YOU HAVE ANY FINAL QUESTIONSSS YOU WISSSH TO ASSSSK?
YEAH, WHAT TIME'S DINNER?
WHAT'S ON THE STONE?
AH, THE SSSTONE... WHY THE LASSST PART OF THE SSSTORY, OF COURSSSE.
SSSHALL I READ IT TO YOU, SSSINCE YOU WILL NEVER ESSSCAPE TO SSSHARE IT WITH ANYONE?
"The great ssserpent's terrible deedsss would become legendary... but its foulessst act remainsss a sssecret."

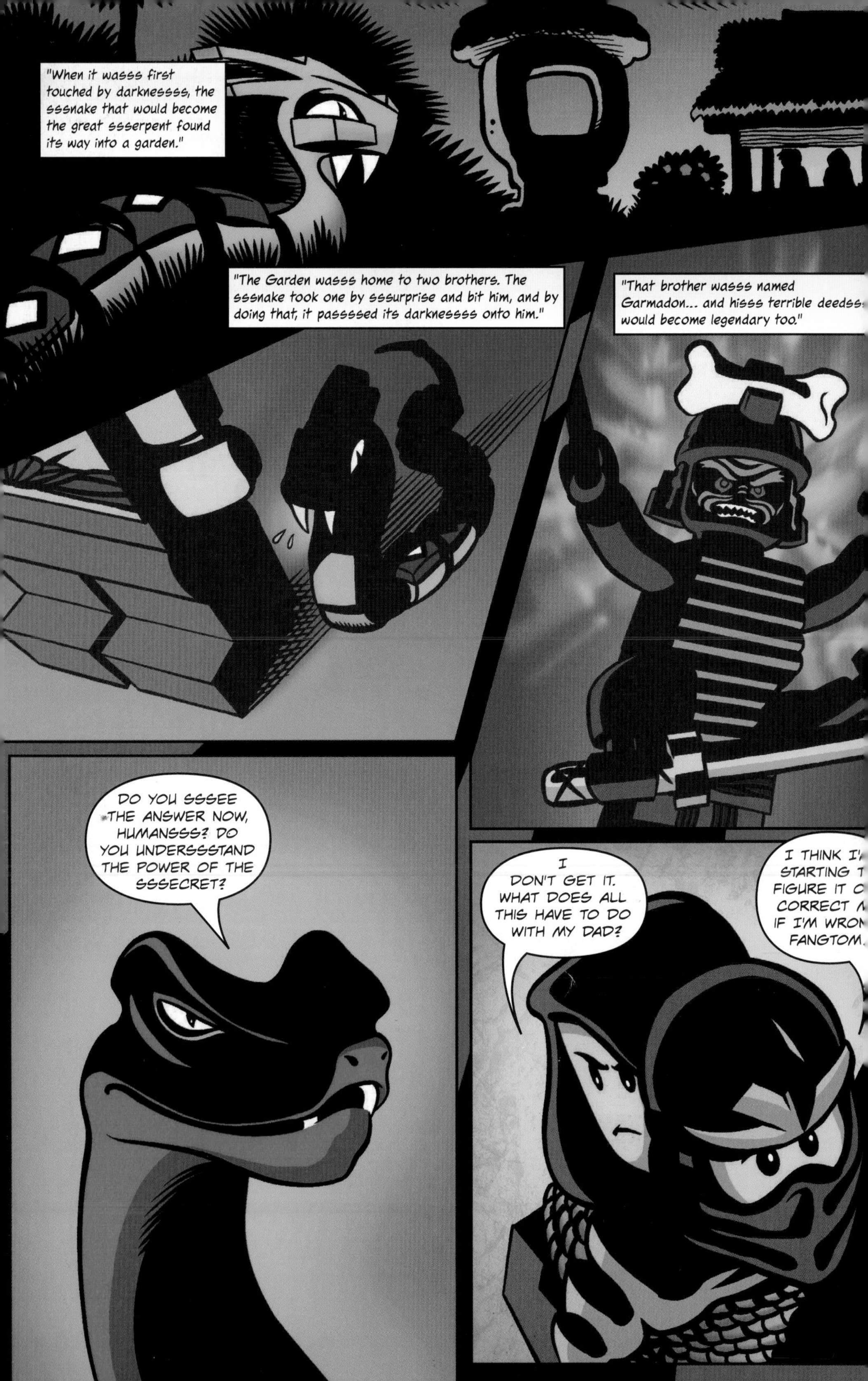
"When it wasss first touched by darknessss, the sssnake that would become the great ssserpent found its way into a garden."
"The Garden wasss home to two brothers. The sssnake took one by sssurprise and bit him, and by doing that, it passssed its darknessss onto him."
"That brother wasss named Garmadon... and hisss terrible deedss would become legendary too."
DO YOU SSSEE THE ANSWER NOW, HUMANSSS? DO YOU UNDERSSSTAND THE POWER OF THE SSSECRET?
I DON'T GET IT. WHAT DOES ALL THIS HAVE TO DO WITH MY DAD?
I THINK I' STARTING T FIGURE IT C CORRECT M IF I'M WRON FANGTOM.

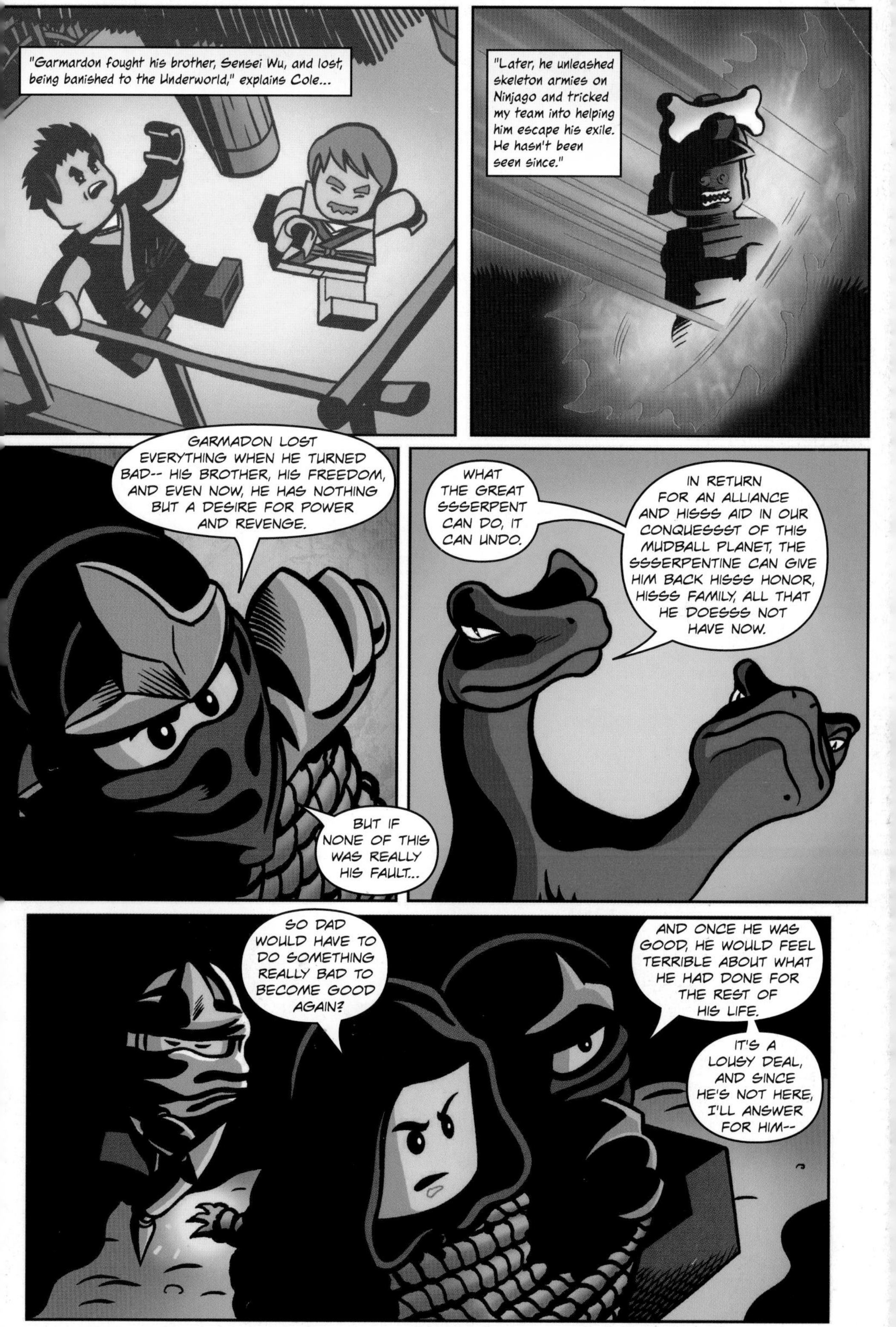
"Garmardon fought his brother, Sensei Wu, and lost, being banished to the Underworld," explains Cole...
"Later, he unleashed skeleton armies on Ninjago and tricked my team into helping him escape his exile. He hasn't been seen since."
GARMADON LOST EVERYTHING WHEN HE TURNED BAD-- HIS BROTHER, HIS FREEDOM, AND EVEN NOW, HE HAS NOTHING BUT A DESIRE FOR POWER AND REVENGE.
BUT IF NONE OF THIS WAS REALLY HIS FAULT...
WHAT THE GREAT SSSERPENT CAN DO, IT CAN UNDO.
IN RETURN FOR AN ALLIANCE AND HISSS AID IN OUR CONQUESSST OF THIS MUDBALL PLANET, THE SSSERPENTINE CAN GIVE HIM BACK HISSS HONOR, HISSS FAMILY, ALL THAT HE DOESSS NOT HAVE NOW.
SO DAD WOULD HAVE TO DO SOMETHING REALLY BAD TO BECOME GOOD AGAIN?
AND ONCE HE WAS GOOD, HE WOULD FEEL TERRIBLE ABOUT WHAT HE HAD DONE FOR THE REST OF HIS LIFE.
IT'S A LOUSY DEAL, AND SINCE HE'S NOT HERE, I'LL ANSWER FOR HIM--

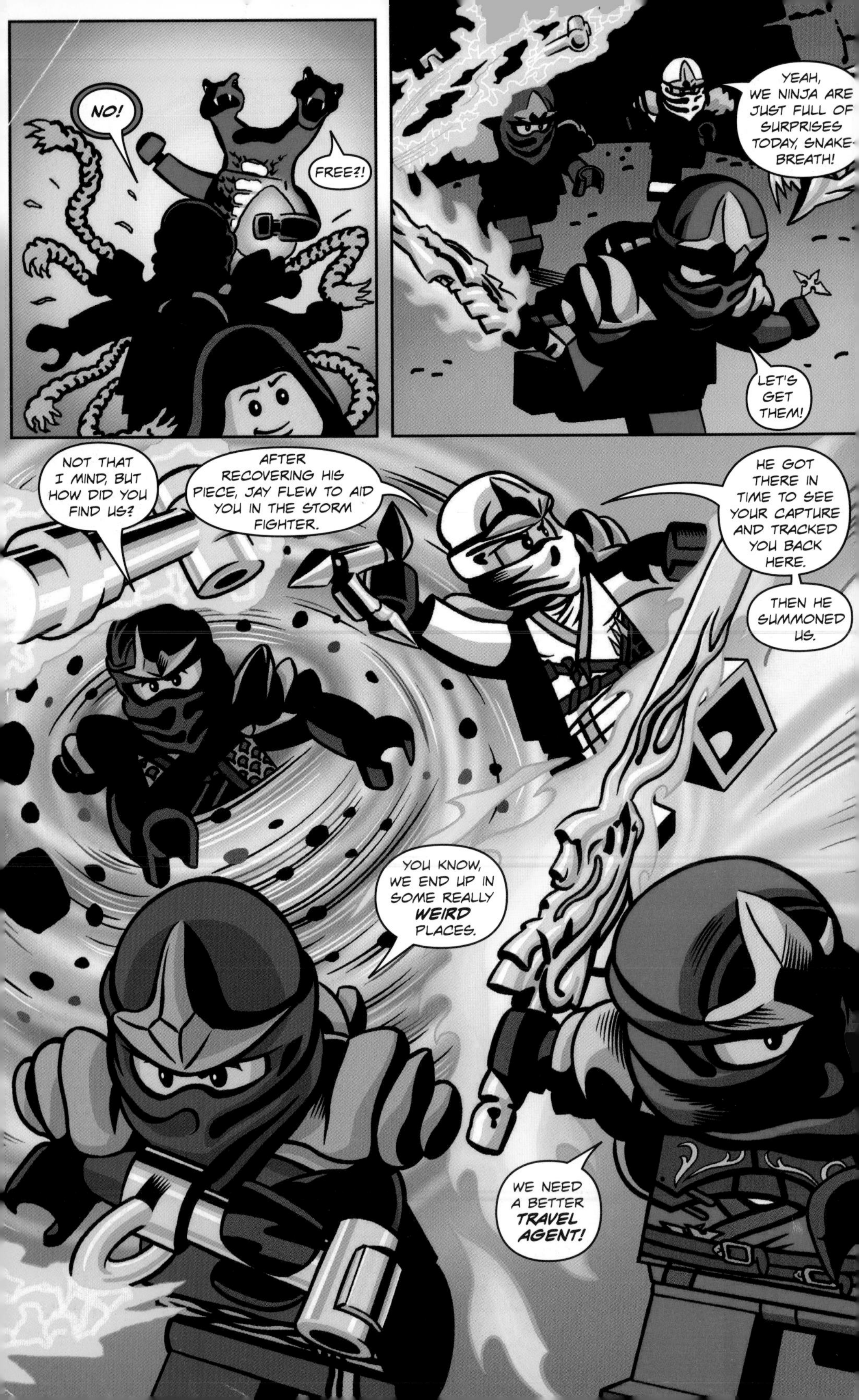

NO!
FREE?!
YEAH, WE NINJA ARE JUST FULL OF SURPRISES TODAY, SNAKE-BREATH!
LET'S GET THEM!
NOT THAT I MIND, BUT HOW DID YOU FIND US?
AFTER RECOVERING HIS PIECE, JAY FLEW TO AID YOU IN THE STORM FIGHTER.
HE GOT THERE IN TIME TO SEE YOUR CAPTURE AND TRACKED YOU BACK HERE.
THEN HE SUMMONED US.
YOU KNOW, WE END UP IN SOME REALLY **WEIRD** PLACES.
WE NEED A BETTER **TRAVEL AGENT!**

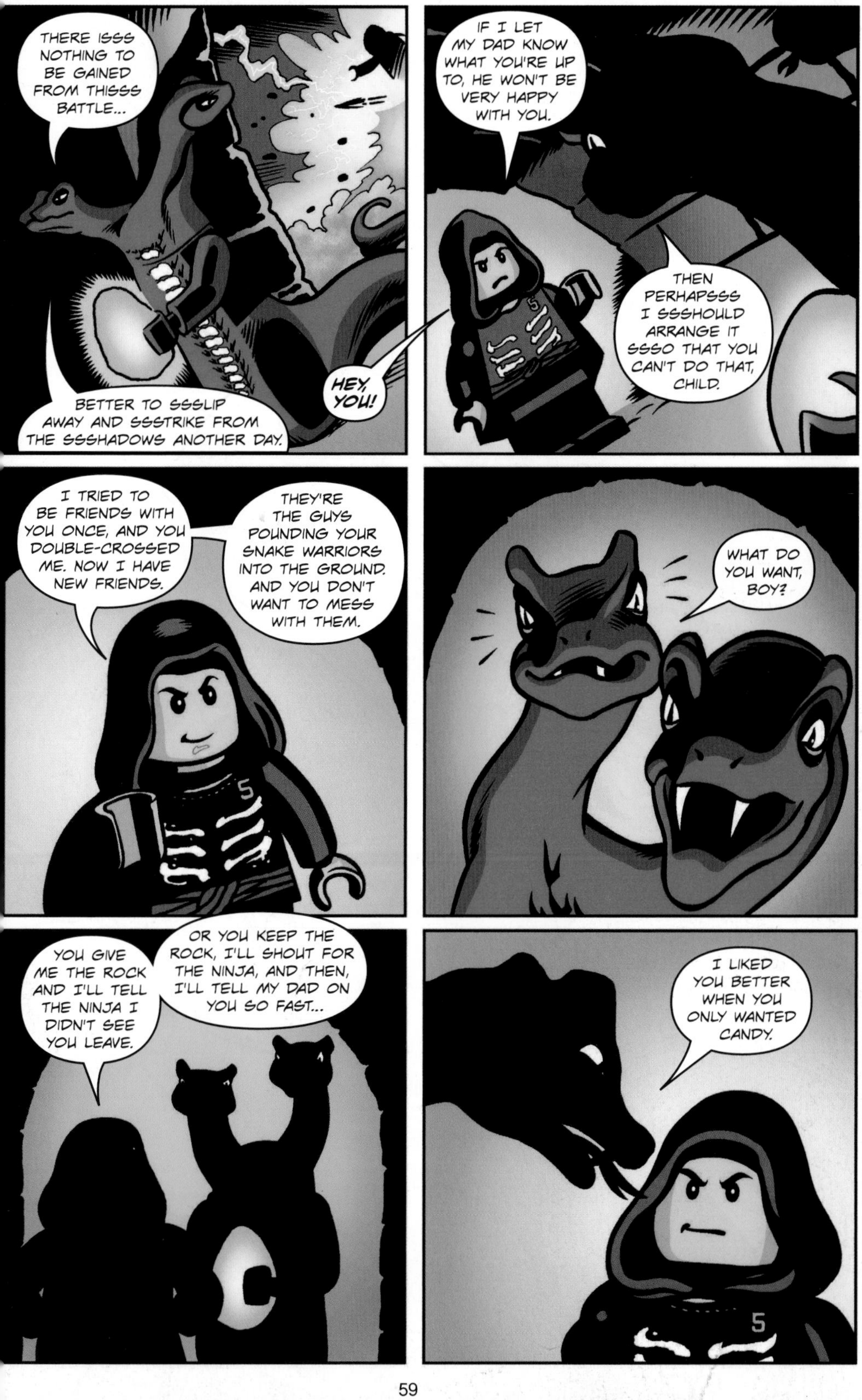
THERE ISSS NOTHING TO BE GAINED FROM THISSS BATTLE...
BETTER TO SSSLIP AWAY AND SSSTRIKE FROM THE SSSHADOWS ANOTHER DAY.
HEY, YOU!
IF I LET MY DAD KNOW WHAT YOU'RE UP TO, HE WON'T BE VERY HAPPY WITH YOU.
THEN PERHAPSSS I SSSHOULD ARRANGE IT SSSO THAT YOU CAN'T DO THAT, CHILD.
I TRIED TO BE FRIENDS WITH YOU ONCE, AND YOU DOUBLE-CROSSED ME. NOW I HAVE NEW FRIENDS.
THEY'RE THE GUYS POUNDING YOUR SNAKE WARRIORS INTO THE GROUND. AND YOU DON'T WANT TO MESS WITH THEM.
WHAT DO YOU WANT, BOY?
YOU GIVE ME THE ROCK AND I'LL TELL THE NINJA I DIDN'T SEE YOU LEAVE.
OR YOU KEEP THE ROCK, I'LL SHOUT FOR THE NINJA, AND THEN, I'LL TELL MY DAD ON YOU SO FAST...
I LIKED YOU BETTER WHEN YOU ONLY WANTED CANDY.

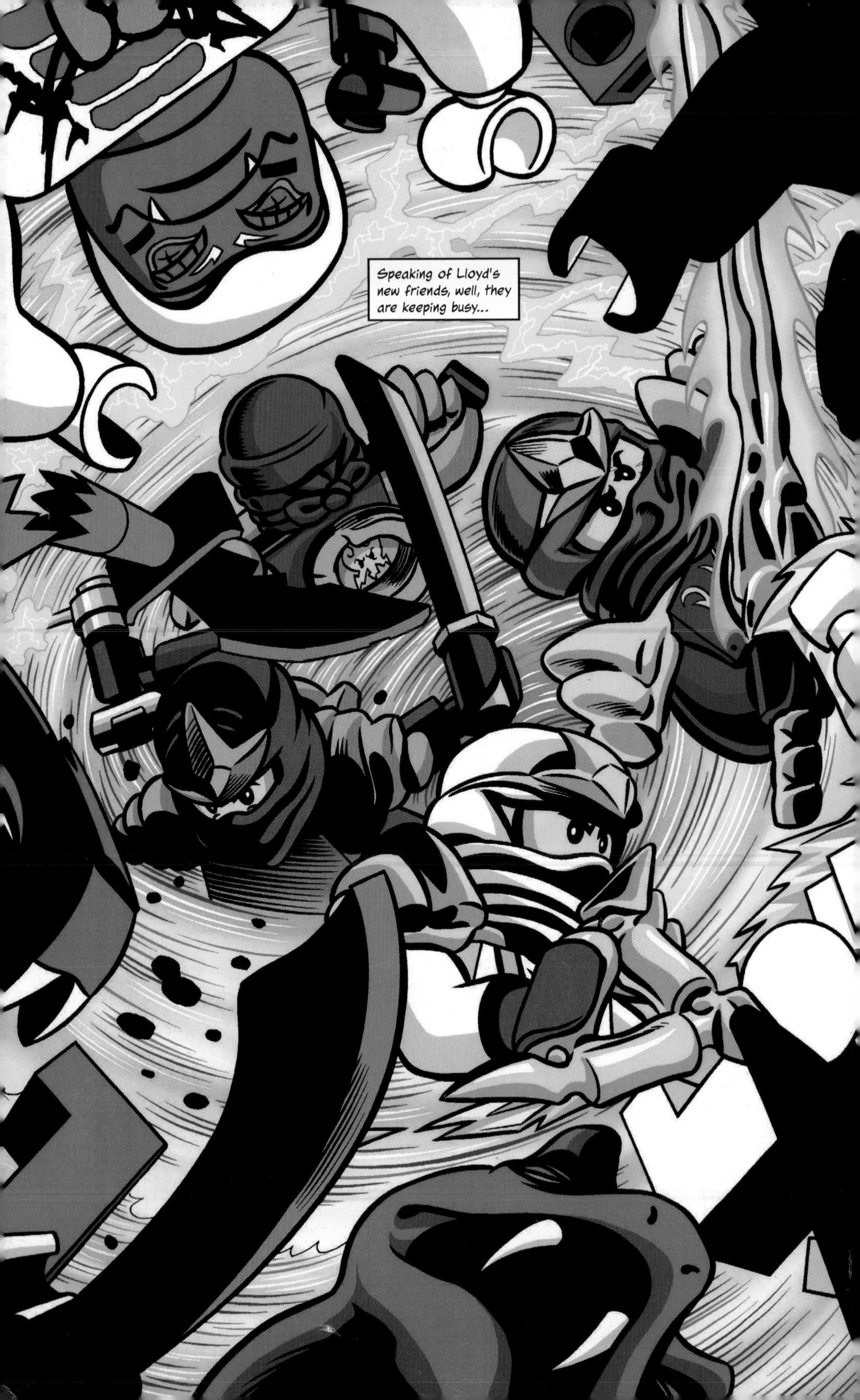
Speaking of Lloyd's new friends, well, they are keeping busy...

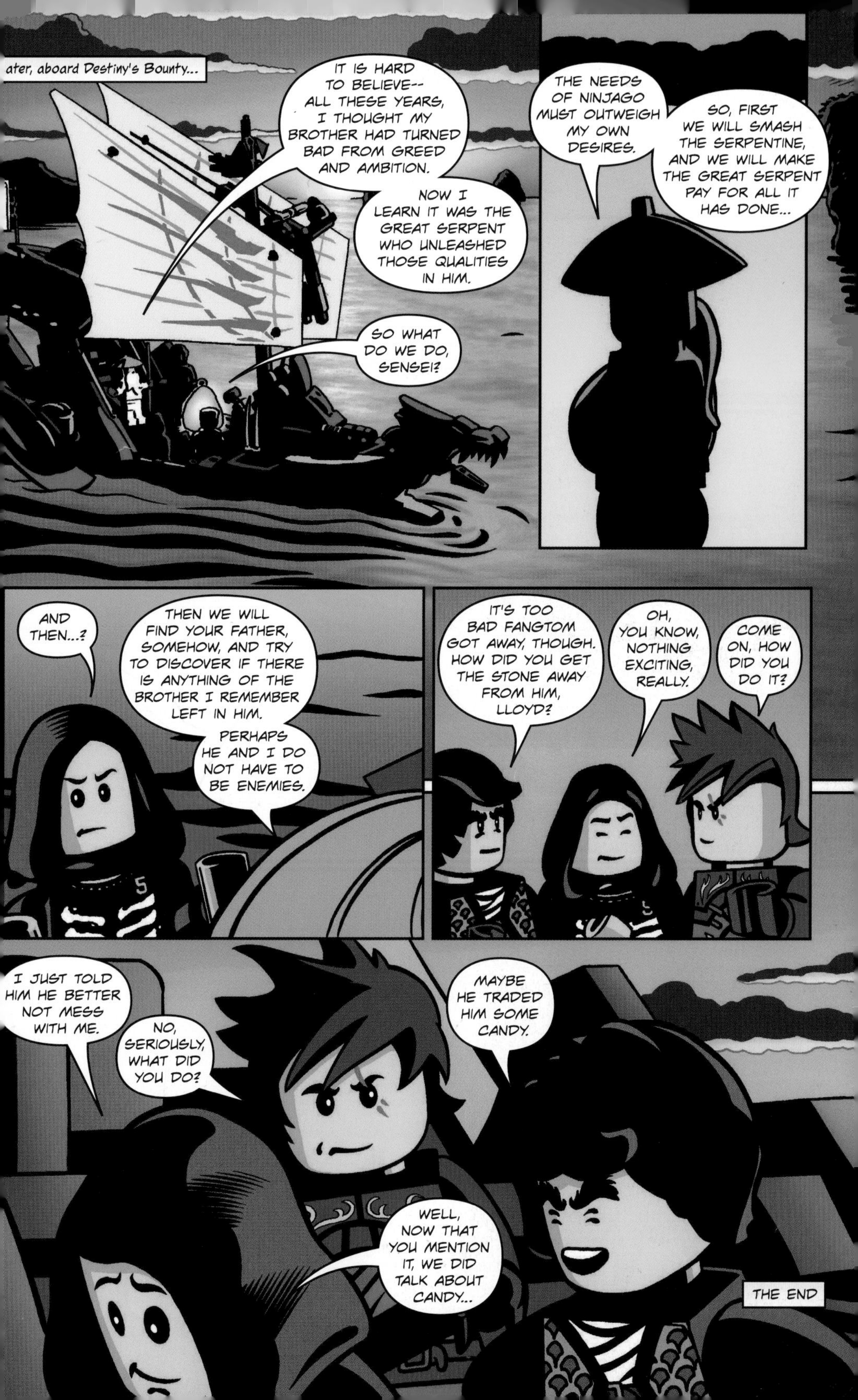
ater, aboard Destiny's Bounty...
IT IS HARD TO BELIEVE-- ALL THESE YEARS, I THOUGHT MY BROTHER HAD TURNED BAD FROM GREED AND AMBITION.
NOW I LEARN IT WAS THE GREAT SERPENT WHO UNLEASHED THOSE QUALITIES IN HIM.
SO WHAT DO WE DO, SENSEI?
THE NEEDS OF NINJAGO MUST OUTWEIGH MY OWN DESIRES.
SO, FIRST WE WILL SMASH THE SERPENTINE, AND WE WILL MAKE THE GREAT SERPENT PAY FOR ALL IT HAS DONE...
AND THEN...?
THEN WE WILL FIND YOUR FATHER, SOMEHOW, AND TRY TO DISCOVER IF THERE IS ANYTHING OF THE BROTHER I REMEMBER LEFT IN HIM.
PERHAPS HE AND I DO NOT HAVE TO BE ENEMIES.
IT'S TOO BAD FANGTOM GOT AWAY, THOUGH. HOW DID YOU GET THE STONE AWAY FROM HIM, LLOYD?
OH, YOU KNOW, NOTHING EXCITING, REALLY.
COME ON, HOW DID YOU DO IT?
I JUST TOLD HIM HE BETTER NOT MESS WITH ME.
NO, SERIOUSLY, WHAT DID YOU DO?
MAYBE HE TRADED HIM SOME CANDY.
WELL, NOW THAT YOU MENTION IT, WE DID TALK ABOUT CANDY...
THE END

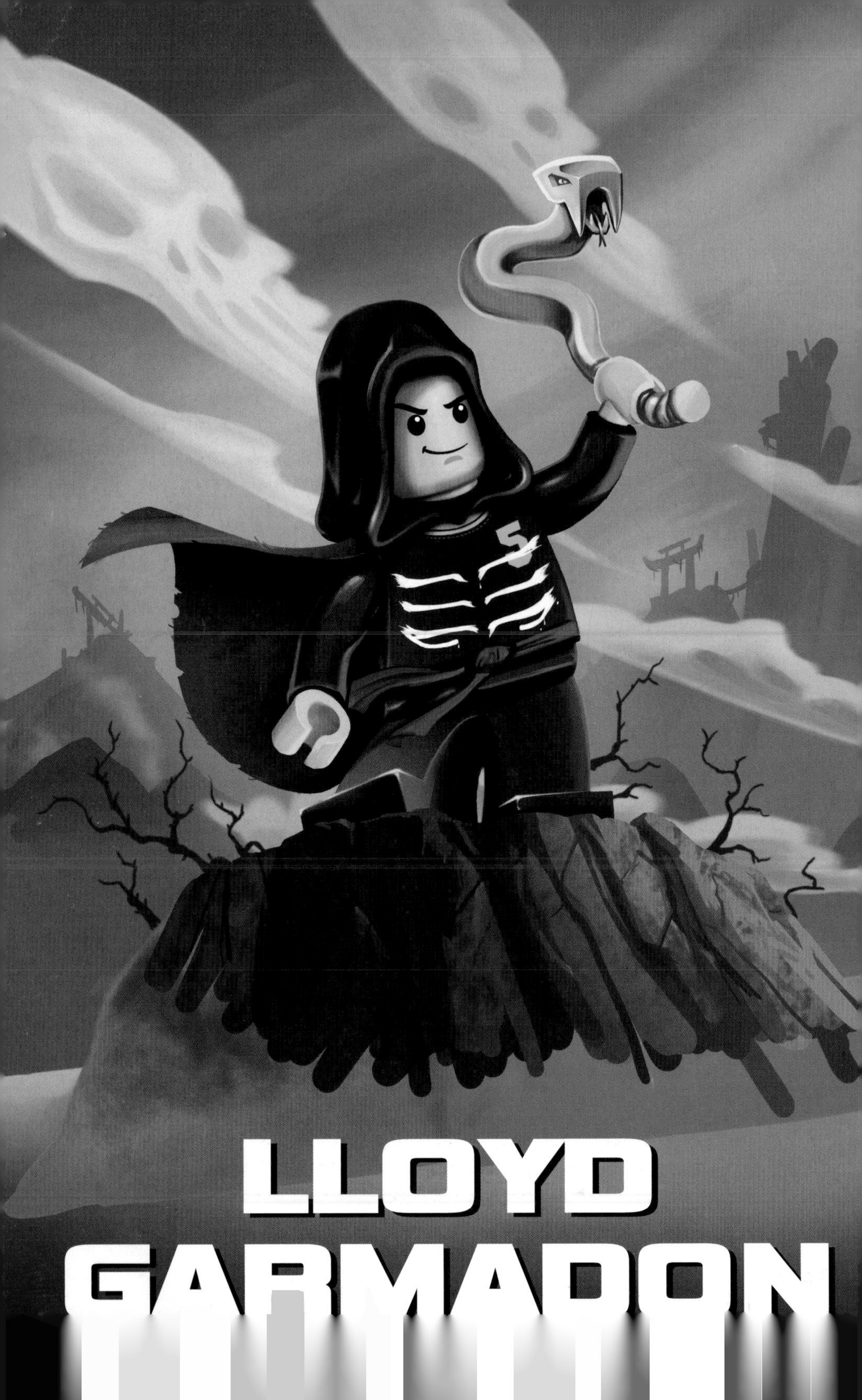
LLOYD
GARMADON

WATCH OUT FOR PAPERCUTZ™

Welcome to the fourth, frightful LEGO® NINJAGO graphic novel from Papercutz, the company dedicated to publishing great graphic novels for all ages. I'm Jim Salicrup, Papercutz Editor-in-Chief and long-time Alice Cooper fan (despite his fondness for snakes). I'm here to tell you all about what's happening behind-the-scenes at Papercutz, and this time I have two really exciting announcements...

First, everyone at Papercutz wants to sincerely thank YOU for helping to make LEGO NINJAGO the best-selling, all-ages graphic novel series for the early part of 2012, and at the rate we're going, possibly for all of 2012! Your support has helped land LEGO NINJAGO #2 "Mask of the Sensei" in the #1 spot on the New York Times Best Selling Graphic Books (paperback) list the week it was released. Since then, both LEGO NINJAGO #1 and #2 have remained in the top ten on that list, and as we go to press, based on advance orders, we suspect both LEGO NINJAGO #3 and #4 will soon be included as well! Again, thank you so much. We greatly appreciate your support.

Photo by James Lew

The other big story is that we have an amazing new artist onboard to draw the LEGO NINJAGO graphic novel series, and his name is JOLYON YATES. Here's just a tiny bit of biographical information on this incredible artist:

Born in England, Jolyon Yates studied graphic design and illustration at Canterbury and Exeter, and Japanese arts in Sapporo, Japan, as a guinea pig in a college exchange program. He lived in Japan for several years, during which time he contributed comics, articles and illustrations to magazines such as *Anime FX*. Jolyon also met his future wife there. He became a US citizen in 2008.

His first paid comics work was the story "Tancho" for *Mangazine*. He completed artwork for the award-winning web comic *Revvvelations* in 2010. Illustration work has included storyboards for commercials and movies and artwork for magazines and animation. He's been a regular contributor to *G-Fan*. He makes a brief appearance in the movie TENGU (2012), for which he drew character designs. He is very happy to be working on LEGO NINJAGO but fears losing the ability to draw fingers, ears, and noses.

So, summing up, LEGO NINJAGO is a hit, and Jolyon Yates will now be bringing Greg Farshtey's amazing scripts to life! And as exciting and action-packed as this graphic novel may be, wait till you see LEGO NINJAGO #5 "Kingdom of the Snakes," coming soon to your favorite booksellers! Till then, don't miss out on any LEGO NINJAGO news, by logging on to www.LEGO.com as often as possible, and stay on top of all the latest news from Papercutz at www.papercutz.com.

So, until next time, keep spinnin'!

Thanks,

Jim

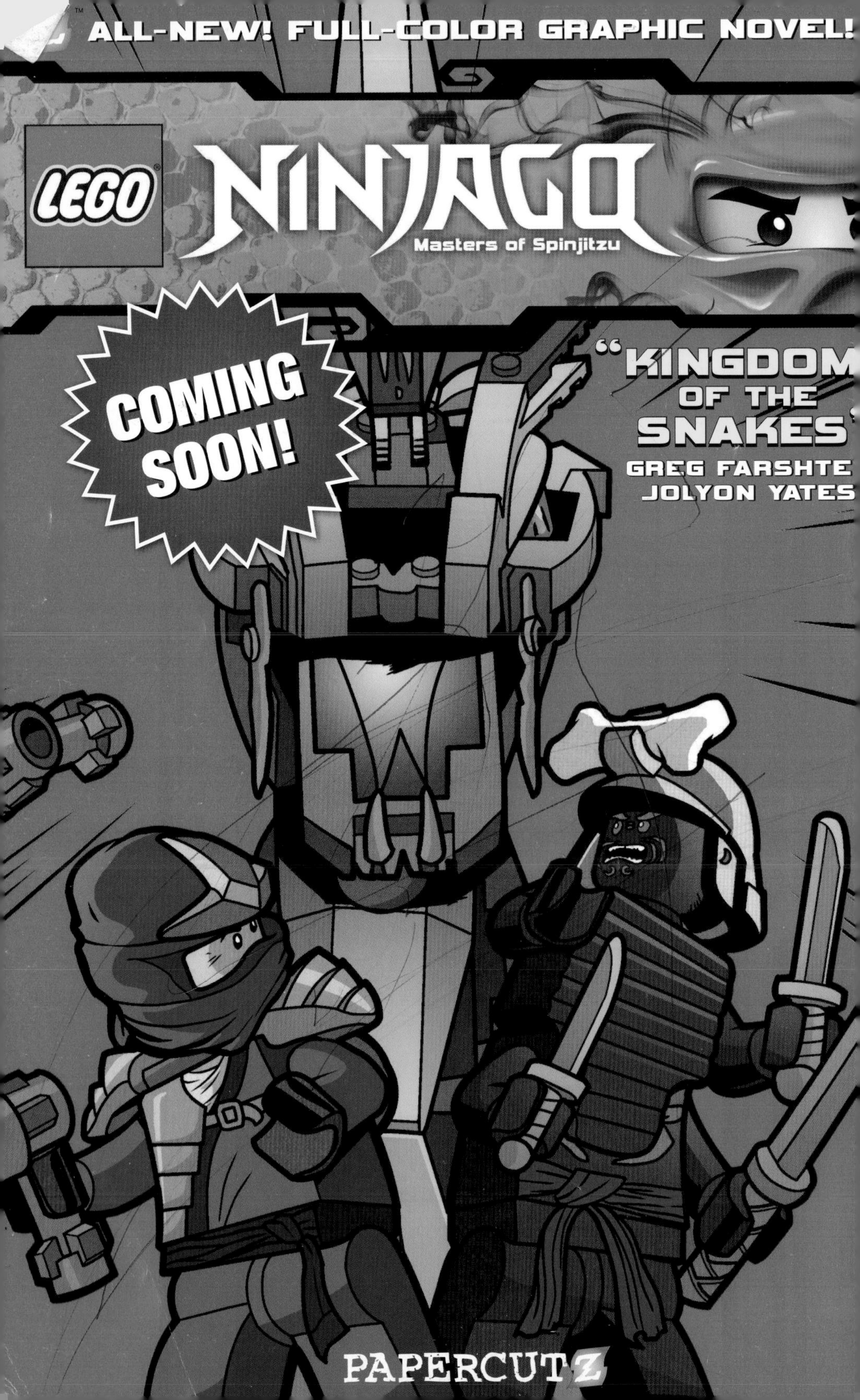
ALL-NEW! FULL-COLOR GRAPHIC NOVEL!
LEGO
NINJAGO
Masters of Spinjitzu
COMING SOON!
"KINGDOM OF THE SNAKES"
GREG FARSHTE
JOLYON YATES
PAPERCUTZ